The Divine Dissimulation

The Divine Zetan Trilogy, Volume 1

Martin Lundqvist

Published by Martin Lundqvist, 2018.

This is a work of fiction. Similarities to real people, places, or events are entirely coincidental.

THE DIVINE DISSIMULATION

First edition. July 20, 2018.

Written by Martin Lundqvist.

Also by Martin Lundqvist

Divine Space Gods
Divine Space Gods: Abraham's Follies
Divine Space Gods II: Revolution for Dummies
Divine Space Gods III: Rangda's Shenanigans

Sabina Saves the Future
Sabina's Pursuit of The Holy Grail
Sabina's Quest to Open the Portal in the Sun Pyramid
Sabina's Expedition to Stop the Apocalypse

The Divine Zetan Trilogy
The Divine Dissimulation
The Divine Sedition
The Divine Finalisation

Standalone
Matt's Amazing Week
James Locker The Duality of Fate
The Portal in the Pyramid
Money Laundering in the Laundromat
Pyramidportalen

Matts Fantastiska Vecka
Divine Space Gods Trilogy
Sabina Saves the Future: Complete Trilogy
Diez Historias Aleatorias y Muy Cortas
Ten Random and Very Short Stories
Dieci Storie Casuali e Molto Brevi
Dix Histoires Aléatoires et Très Courtes
Zehn Zufällige und Sehr Kurze Geschichten
Cinco Historias Aleatorias y Muy Cortas
Five Random and Very Short Stories
The Fall of Martin Orchard
Masa Depan Putri Sabina
La Caída de Martin Orchard
The Banker and The Dragon

Watch for more at martinlundqvist.com.

Chapter 1 Introduction

Abraham Goldstein was looking out through the windows of the 3000 meters high Goldstein Tower built in the centre of Antarctica. The Goldstein Tower was the second largest structure on Earth built in a pyramid shape to support its tremendous weight and to make the building secure from attacks. From the top of Goldstein Tower Abraham Goldstein could see all his domains, the lush farmlands, the vast, serene parks, and the residential complexes where his loyal followers lived. Abraham sighed, despite owning all of this he was not satisfied, he wanted to own more, and be more powerful.

Being 250 years old, Abraham hoped that his DNA was possible to regenerate once more so that he would feel like a young man again. Abraham knew there were no guarantees, as he was on the fringes of what was achievable with the DNA regeneration technology. Regardless of what he did death was crawling closer.

Abraham exhaled and relaxed. Tomorrow would be a momentous day, and if he had lived for 250 years, he would survive another day.

Abraham was excited for the next morning because of reports that the Divine Detection program was ready. He had ordered his scientists that he wanted to be the first person to use the innovative technology. Hopefully, it would answer all his questions about God and make him meet the divine being.

The Divine Detection program was the latest marvel of quantum physics and a top-secret project of House Goldstein. It scanned through the dimensional layers of reality, and if it found the Divine Dimension, it could transport the consciousness of the user there, so he could meet the divine beings while still being alive.

Wanting to meet God with a fresh mind, Abraham entered the sleeping pod in his bedroom, set it to four hours, and instantly fell asleep.

Chapter 2: The Solar System In 2785

In 2785 most of the solar system was inhabited. Mars was the major population centre with 4 billion inhabitants. Earth had only 1 billion inhabitants, and they were living their life in abundance as Terran Citizens owned almost everything in the solar system.

Earth's limited population was because the ruling Terran Council in the 23rd century decreed the sterilisation or deportation of everyone who was not rich or had exceptional genes. Most people chose sterilization, living out their lives peacefully while others had left Earth. Since the 24th century, the population of Earth stayed stable around 1 billion, which was the ideal population to avoid civil conflict and resource shortfall.

In 2785 every birth and death on Earth were tightly regulated, and no natural conceptions occurred. Instead, citizens had to apply to have children. If approved, scientific DNA optimisation ensured that every individual had the best possible genes. Individuals who were wealthy could usually apply to have more than one child, while poor people and people with undesired genetics had to leave the planet if they wanted offspring.

The Terran Council controlled the weather on Earth, through launching large mirrors and shades orbiting Earth. The mirrors increased the amount of sunshine on the surface making cold areas such as Antarctica warmer, while the shades decreased the amount of sunshine making the surface cooler in the tropical regions.

Technically, the planet Earth was still divided into different countries, but they had lost their meaning as all the political and economic power was with the major company conglomerates. The five large conglomerates governed Earth via The Terran Council, which consisted of:

- House Goldstein that ruled Antarctica, Australia, and South America;
- House White that ruled North America;

- House Muller that ruled Europe;
- House Rashid that ruled the Middle East and Africa
- House Cheng that ruled most of the Asian continent.

Through the Terran Council, the major factions met and made sure that life on Earth was plentiful and peaceful. There had been peace on Earth through the Pax Terran agreement for 300 years. Outside of Earth, however, the Terran factions were always fighting each other indirectly through supporting different sides in proxy wars on other planets.

All the major population centres on Earth were connected by a network of trains that ran in vacuum tubes and could reach speeds of up to 10,000 kilometres an hour. This way all the major cities could reach each other within an hour or two.

Mars in 2785 was a chaotic poverty-stricken planet full of warring factions. When Mars was terraformed 500 years earlier, it was intended for a maximum of 200 million people, and now it had 20 times more people. The excessive population meant that water and other natural resources were limited. The only things that seemed to exist in abundance were weapons and synthetic drugs.

Despite its imperfections, many of the Martians still loved the Martian lifestyle, as it was freer than the Terran one. On Mars, people could live like they wanted, while everything was tightly regulated on Earth. Freedom came at a price though, as the life expectancy on Mars was 40 years while it was 150 years on Earth. Abraham Goldstein who was 250 years old was the oldest man on Earth as he was wealthy and could get his scientists to extend his life a lot longer than most people.

Life on Mars could have been better if the Terran Council had not feared the Martian way of life, and intentionally kept the planet weak. The trading terms between the planets were extremely unbalanced, and the Terran Council took whatever they wanted from Mars paying next to nothing. The Terran Council extorted the Martians, intimidating them with the superior Terran technology and creating mayhem when the Martians dared to resist.

Export of Terran technology to Mars was not allowed, so most Martians had only access to 500-year-old technology. If the Terran Council wanted to, they could have given Martian population a safe atmosphere protecting them from the toxic stellar background radiation. Instead, these resources were spent on having a massive military fleet orbiting Mars to show the Martians who were the masters of the solar system.

Humans had evolved differently on different planets. The people on Earth were all picture perfect due to the genetic pre-selection. Depending on the culture they could be athletic or lean, but in all cultures, they had ideal complexion and ideal posture. They were highly intelligent humanoids but also highly obedient and non-questioning as that was how the ruling classes liked their subjects. The Martian human genome had defects from radiation and genetic mutation. Most Martians looked sickly and were genetically predisposed for artificial drug addictions. On the flipside, they were radiation, virus, and infection resistant and a lot more resilient than their Terran counterparts.

Because of their radiation resistance, Martians were employed to do dangerous jobs in the solar system such as building and maintaining the automated mining stations on Jupiter's moons and building asteroid mining stations. A lot of them smuggled Terran technology back to Mars, so the expeditions hiring Martians was not allowed to use new technology due to the paranoia of the Terran Council. The Martian laborers were always supervised under close Terran military supervision.

Among other inhabited places in the solar system; Venus was only used for its automated mines and prison camps where condemned prisoners lived in endless darkness and suffering. Life expectancy for anyone residing on Venus was less than 15 years. Likewise, Mercury was too close to the sun to terraform properly for human settlement.

Many of the asteroids were used by wealthy Terrans as holiday houses. This was because the technology existed that could put them in any selected orbit around the sun, with artificial atmosphere and artificial gravity. A lot of asteroids also orbited Earth as holiday houses for wealthy Terrans.

Finally, a few planets orbiting other stars had human colonies. While the technology existed to travel this far, the Terran Council did not see it as viable investments. The fastest travel speed possible with the available technology was $1/10^{th}$ of the speed of light, which meant that it took at least 40 years to reach Alpha Centauri B, the closest star. While it was possible to travel this far by cryogenically freezing the crew before the trip, it was not profitable to do so, as it was impossible to control the inhabitants of colonies on Alpha Centauri as it took four years to send them a message and 40 years to travel there.

Thus, all the colonies outside the solar system, was founded by eccentric trillionaires with no heirs and no better use for their money. These colonies were independent and had very limited contact with Earth.

Chapter 3 The Divine Suicide and Ascension Plan

Abraham Goldstein woke up four hours later. He was full of energy. He took the elevator 800 levels down, to a top-secret research lab 300 meters below ground. It was so secret that not even his family members knew about it. Abraham met up with Jack Brown, the lead scientist for the project. Abraham:

- Is the machine ready?

Jack:

- Yes, it should be operational now. I must warn you though, we haven't tested the device yet and it might be dangerous.

Abraham:

- And you are not going to test the machine for that matter. I am not spending 80 billion Terran Credits on a scientist's toy; this is MY toy!

The 80 billion Terran Credits devoted to the Divine Detector machine was an absolute fortune. The construction of the entire 3000 meters high Goldstein tower had cost 120 billion Terran Credits, and that was an 800-level building with 16,000 rooms.
Jack:

- Understood, sir! We have scanned the entire spectra of potential dimensions, and we believe that the one you are looking for is located at the coordinates Gamma; Omega; Delta; one; nine; eight; five.

Abraham:

- Excellent, plug me in.

Jack:

- Okay, I'll keep you in the Divine Dimension for just a few seconds. You'll experience it as a lot longer as we predict that time moves very slowly in there.

Jack Brown started the Divine Detector particle accelerator, and Abraham Goldstein could feel that his consciousness left his body. He was travelling through space at speed faster than light. In the blink of an eye, Abraham crashed down into an open courtyard.

Abraham got up and studied the courtyard. It was both beautiful and eerie at the same time. He looked at a pond full of lotus flowers. In the reflection of the pond, he could see the Goldstein Tower below as if he was on a floating structure high up in the sky. Abraham was stunned by fascination, but he snapped out of it. He was here with a purpose; to meet God. Abraham saw a big gate at the end of the courtyard, and his gut feeling told him it was the right way. He walked through the gate, and he entered a throne room. At the far end of the room, there was a golden throne full of gemstones. The gemstones radiated with an intense light.

After marvelling at the beauty of the throne for a while, Abraham saw a dead man in robes lying on the ground; facing down. Abraham approached the lifeless body and turned it around. He looked at it in awe. The corpse belonged to Yahweh the god of his people. But Yahweh was dead? How could this be?

After the initial shock, Abraham knew that he had to find a reason behind Yahweh's death. He searched the clothes of the dead deity, and he found a letter. It was written in an ancient language, but Abraham instinctively understood the meaning of the message. The letter said;

"This is how I end my life, with a knife to my throat. I thought that being the sole ruler of humanity was all I ever wanted, so I expelled the other divines from my palace after murdering Lucifer, my best friend and lover. Unfortunately, I destroyed the portal to Earth in the altercation with the other Zetans. I am lonely

and battling with guilt and my demons. Humanity does not need me anymore, and I don't feel the need to live either. This is my end.

Yours Truly

Yahweh

PS. Since you are reading this, humanity obviously needs a god. Take my place! Go to the altar, to the left of my throne and you'll know how."

Abraham got up and he walked to the altar. What he saw fascinated him. On the altar, he saw a blueprint for three different microchips:

- The top chip was the god chip; it allowed the user to connect with and communicate with up to 10,000 followers at a time. It also enabled the user to directly control the actions of anyone with an angel chip implanted. The God chip also had the feature that the one wearing it, could instantly kill anyone with an angel or human chip implanted.
- The middle chip was the angel chip. It allowed the user to connect with up to 100 followers at the time.
- The bottom chip was the human chip. It made it possible for gods and angels to enter the mind of anyone having the chip implanted in their brain and communicates with them.

Abraham memorised the schematics, using the bionic memory enhancing microchip he had implanted in his brain. The world then blurred in front of his eyes, and he was back in the research lab of Goldstein Tower.

Jack Brown approached Abraham as he came back to consciousness:

- Did you find what you were looking for?

Abraham:

- No, but I found something else.
- Can you extract three schematics from my memory?

Jack:

- Yes, wait a second.
- Yes, I got them.

- Do you know what they are?

Abraham:

- Yes, but that is none of your business.
- All I need to know is whether you can make them?

Jack:

- Yes, with our particle replicator machine we can replicate any item we have a blueprint of, including those schematics.

Abraham:

- Good.

- I want one microchip of the top schematic plan and 300 microchips of the bottom plan. Have them done by tomorrow.

- And make sure this stays between us, for your families' sake.

Jack:

- Yes, sir! Consider it done, sir!

Abraham left the room, and Jack sighed. He felt worried. Although he was an agnostic, humans should not try to reach the divine realm. What was the story with these microchips? What had happened when Abraham was connected to the machine? Jack Brown had never seen any microchips like these schematics before, and he could only guess what they would do. Regardless, Jack would do as Abraham had ordered and produce the batch. He owed Abraham that.

A decade earlier, Jack Brown had done the unthinkable and fallen in love with a Martian woman during a House White research expedition on Mars. When Benjamin White, the director of the Mars expedition found out about the love affair, he condemned Jack Brown's entire research team, consisting of 16 researchers and revoked their Terran citizenships. He did this, as House

White was the most racist of the Terran factions, and it showed their people on Earth that it was not okay for anyone to have relations with Martians.

Unfortunately for Benjamin White, his move to banish House White's foremost quantum physicists over a race matter was not appreciated by his peers, and he was assassinated later that year. By that time there was no trace of the team, and it took House White years to find out that Abraham Goldstein had hired Jack Brown.

Fortunately, for Jack and his staff; Abraham was more pragmatic than racist, and he offered them safe re-entry to Earth as well as new Terran citizenships if they worked for him. He even promised Jack Brown that he could have children with his Martian wife and that both she and the children would be granted Terran citizenships by Abraham when the project finished.

With no time to waste, Jack gathered his team to make the microchips requested by Abraham. It would be a challenging task, but luckily, they were all experts at using the particle replicator machine, and they had access to every element possible.

Chapter 4: Abraham Goldstein Makes New Plans.

Abraham Goldstein sat in his penthouse reflecting over the past day's event. It was a shame that Yahweh was dead, as Abraham had so much respect for him and wanted to learn everything from the great creator. But Yahweh's death had opened the opportunity for Abraham to reach a higher goal, to be greater than any man before him, to be immortal, to become a god. This was his destiny; it wasn't chance that led him to the Divine Dimension, it was providence. Yahweh wanted Abraham to be his successor and it was his duty to comply.

But first, he had to find out if the divine microchip worked. The god version of the chip was big and bulky as it needed to be able to communicate with up to 10,000 followers at a time. To protect it, Abraham had ordered Jack Brown to forge it into a golden crown. Abraham put on the crown and screamed in pain as the microchip merged with his brain, and the crown was stuck into place. A young and beautiful female servant came rushing in.

Servant:

- Are you okay sir; I heard a loud scream?

Abraham:

- I have never been better.

Servant:

- That's excellent sir. May I ask about the golden crown, I have never seen you wear it before?

Abraham:

- You are not paid to ask questions! Be gone!

Abraham clenched his teeth in frustration after the servant left. He used to sleep with his servants when he was younger and more virile. He still wanted to keep up the illusion that he had sex with his servants, so he hired young and beautiful girls to be his aides. The truth was that he had not had sex for the last 100 years. He just could not feel physical attraction anymore. His doctors had told him this was a common side effect of the DNA regenerations technology; that many people could not feel sexual attraction after their natural lifespan ended.

Abraham thought of his former wife, Lillian Goldstein, who died 130 years earlier. She had refused DNA regeneration technology claiming that if God had wanted her to live longer, he would have given her better genes, and artificially extending one's life led to misery. Abraham mourned Lillian's death, and he was unable to love anyone else; thus, he was very lonely.

Abraham got back to the matter at hand. The divine golden crown caused him an excruciating headache, but it didn't give spiritual clarity and supernatural insights. He realised that the purpose of the God chip wasn't to provide in-depth knowledge but merely to control the subjects below him. Thus, he needed to test the Human chip, and fortunately there was a suitable candidate.

Abraham's inner circle, the Angels, had caught a suspected spy from House Cheng earlier in the day. This spy would be the ideal test subject for the human chip, as he would be killed anyway. With no time to waste, Abraham took the elevator down to another basement level of Goldstein tower, to the premises of the Angel program.

Chapter 5: A Successful Test

Wilfred Zhang was terrified. He was gravely wounded, and he understood that he would never see his family again. The worst part was that he was completely innocent of the allegations. He had travelled to Antarctica to negotiate a trade deal for a minor independent Chinese company. Suddenly, masked men had knocked him unconscious and moved him to this dark room.

Wilfred looked up. He was surprised when he saw a familiar face in front of him, the face of Abraham Goldstein. Wilfred was baffled; he could never have imagined that the leader of a major faction came down to oversee the torture of a prisoner. Abraham signalled to the guards to hold Wilfred while he pressed something into his ear. After that, they all left without saying a word.

In the next room, Abraham observed Wilfred and felt excited. The Human chip had merged with Wilfred's brain stem. The technology worked; he could feel what Wilfred felt, he could see what Wilfred saw, and he could read his mind. Poor Wilfred; he wasn't a spy just an innocent man petrified of his imminent death. *"Oh well I can sort you out,"* Abraham thought and started transmitting to Wilfred

Abraham (As a voice in Wilfred's head)

- Wilfred, Wilfred can you hear me.
- This is God; I can show you the path out of here.

Wilfred (screaming out loud):

- What? What is this, what are you doing to me?

Abraham:

- Don't question, just believe, and follow the path

Wilfred:

- Okay God, please show me the path

Abraham:

- Good, you'll be rewarded.
- You'll see your family again, and the pain will be gone.

Having said this, Abraham induced a hallucination into the brain of Wilfred. While hallucinating, Wilfred thought he was at home with his family and the pain was gone. It didn't last for long, as Abraham got distracted when Lucifer and Metatron, from his ANGEL program, talked among themselves:
Lucifer:

- What the heck is happening? What is he doing?

Metatron:

- I have no idea

Abraham:

- Don't worry gentlemen. Everything is working exactly as it should. This man is innocent. I want you to detain him until I instruct you otherwise.

- Make sure he gets medical attention at once; I don't want him dead.

Abraham left the room, and the flabbergasted Lucifer and Metatron sat quiet for a long time trying to figure out what had just happened.

Chapter 6: More Test Subjects Are Acquired

Abraham Goldstein was back in his Penthouse in Goldstein Tower. He marvelled over the day's successful technology test. The Divine Technology was divine inspiration and not imagination nor insanity. Given that divine technology worked, that would imply that everything else he had experienced in the Divine Dimension was also genuine and not a product of his imagination.

Abraham had noticed that he had struggled to focus his mind to control the mind of the person below him. As soon as he got distracted, he lost the connection, and the power over the test subject's mind was lost. While controlling the mind of one individual at the time was useful, it hardly made him a divine being, so he had to step up his performance as the divine chip was meant to control up to 10,000 people at the same time.

The first step would be to connect more test subjects. Abraham was thinking of getting his Angels to acquire new subjects, but he realised that there was a much easier way. His female assistants had a clause in their contracts that they were to satisfy his sexual desires if requested. It was time to activate that clause and give them the time of their lives at the same time. Abraham had eight female assistants, and this evening Jenny Lundberg from Northern Europe was the one on duty. He called her on the intercom asking her to come over in a sexy dress.

A bit later, she arrived in the room. Jenny seemed anxious and reluctant. She had been hired for over three years, and Abraham had during this time never used any sexual innuendo. Asking her to come in a sexy dress was different from his usual self. The Abraham she that knew liked to spend hours reading ancient tomes in solitude and silence.

Abraham Goldstein:

- Hello Jenny. I have summoned you to honour clause 6.6 of your employment contract.

Jenny Lundberg (speaking nervously)

- He-he I don't know what that means. I haven't read the contract since I started.

Abraham Goldstein:

- It means that you and I are going to have sex tonight.
- Come here, I don't like asking twice!

Jenny stood petrified, and she did not know what to do. Abraham decided that he did not have the time to wait, so he walked up to her and pressed the human chip into her ear. She felt a sharp pain, but soon she forgot about the pain as she became head over heel aroused. The next 25 minutes she had sex that was out of this world with the oldest man on the planet. Or at least, that was what Jenny thought. In reality, Abraham was sitting on a couch with an excellent scotch controlling her hallucination.

Although Abraham for the first time in 100 years felt some sexual arousal, he chose not to act on it. His body was an old vessel with not much time left; it would be unwise to risk losing his future immortality trying to please something that was going to disappear soon anyway.

Chapter 7: Abraham Returns to The Divine Dimension

A few days later, Abraham Goldstein was in the basement level where the Divine Detector machine was found. He had managed to implant the human chip into six out of eight assistants. The last two had stormed off when Abraham requested sex and mentioned the contract. It wasn't a big deal; he would just have to fire them.

The purpose of Abraham's trip back to the Divine Dimension was to see if he could control multiple subjects at the same time. An hour in the Divine Dimension was equivalent to a second in the real world so with a bit of luck he would be able to control several subjects at the same time without losing connection. He had arranged so that all his six assistants would be at the spa in his penthouse. They would all get an experience out of this world today. He connected to each of them, and yes, they were all waiting for him in the spa. *"Good girls,"* he thought and smiled.

Jack Brown and few of his team members walked in. Jack approached Abraham:

Jack:

- I brought some more people today.

- 20 minutes in there will feel like 50 days if what you are saying is correct.

Abraham:

- So, I get 50 days from 20 minutes? That sounds like an excellent way to extend my life.

Jack:

- There is one problem, the immense amount of energy that the machine uses.

Abraham:

- I got your memo; I have ordered all non-essential production to shut down for the next 30 minutes.

Jack:

- A lot of people will complain.

Abraham:

- Yes, but that's my problem and not yours.
- I don't have time for more questions.
- Start the machine

A moment later, Abraham arrived in the Divine Dimension. He took a seat under a lotus tree and tried connect with all the subjects at once. Success! From the Divine Dimension, he could Control the minds of several individuals at once. Abraham felt like a god. He invoked himself and his subjects into an orgasmic trance. He could feel how days and nights passed by as he was engulfed by the transcendental feelings of spirituality and desire. In the blink of an eye, he was back in the divine detector lab.
Jack:

- You look blissful...

Abraham:

- Yes...

- Turn on the production again; I don't want my whiny grandson to complain about lost money.

Chapter 8: CEO Meeting with Jake Goldstein.

Jake Goldstein was furious. He had requested an explanation from his grandfather, Abraham Goldstein, why all the production had been stopped earlier during the day. Abraham had nonchalantly told him that he was welcome to swing by his penthouse if he wanted to talk.

As Jake arrived at the elevator, there was a notice saying that the elevator was turned off to save power, but Jake was more than welcome to walk up. As Jake's office was located 20 levels below Abraham's penthouse, it was a lot of stairs to climb. Jake Goldstein was 190 years old and he resembled his grandfather in having almost relentless energy, especially when angered. Huffing and puffing he reached the top level of Goldstein Tower. Abraham was sitting in the spa with one of his assistants and flanked by several bodyguards.

Abraham greeted his grandson arrogantly:

- Greetings grandson, you don't look to well, did you have a nice walk.

After a while, Jake finally caught his breath.

- You bastard! You made me WALK 20 levels!

Abraham:

- Yes, exercise is good for you, and besides, I reckoned we needed to save power to get our production up.

Jake:

- Ha-ha very funny
- Now tell me why on earth you turned off production for half an hour?

- Do you even realise how expensive that is?

Abraham:

- Is this trivia time? Very well.

- I turned off the production because I needed extra power for my secret research project.

- It costs us 1.2 million Terran Credits per minute to turn off production, so I would say around 36 million for the half an hour.

Jake:

- WHAT is our secret research project? Shouldn't I, the CEO, know what is costing us all this money? We are losing money for the first time in company history.

Abraham:

- Dear Grandson. You are the CEO because you are my oldest living descendant and I can't be bothered with day-to-day operations anymore.

- Our secret research program has made a significant breakthrough, and I will showcase it at the annual general meeting next week.

- I am turning on the elevator for you to save your legs.

- Guards, show Jake to the elevator, please.

After Jake had left the penthouse level, Abraham told his female assistant and security guards to leave him alone. He preferred solitude, so he could think without unnecessary distractions. Abraham had felt compelled to give Jake a display as he hated when people questioned him.

Abraham disliked most of his descendants and extended family members. And there were a lot of them! As Abraham had lived for 250 years, he had ten generations below him. As the Goldstein's were the wealthiest family in the world, they all qualified to have a lot of children, and all these generations, had spouses. In total the living members of Abraham's extended family accounted to 300 individuals, and sadly the only one's Abraham had liked was his wife and his children, and they had all died of age and sickness.

Chapter 9: Annual General of Meeting House Goldstein

Abraham Goldstein was sitting on the golden throne in the Divine Dimension meditating. Abraham was waiting for the annual general meeting of House Goldstein to begin. The 300 largest shareholders, mostly family members were expected to come for the proceedings, which were held in the main auditorium of Goldstein Tower.

Abraham had a surprise for his family members! The days before the meeting, his Angels had secretly implanted a Divine Technology Human chips into everyone's head. This was done night-time after spraying in in sleep-inducing gas in the rooms of the delegates. As the gas had sedative properties, Abraham hoped that no one had noticed the pain when the chip merged with the brain stem.

For the first time since Abraham found the Divine Dimension, he felt annoyed. Since a second in the real world was equivalent to an hour in the Divine Dimension, it was not an easy waiting for the last stragglers to get to the meeting. Abraham felt like he had been waiting for weeks and this was angering him.

Eventually, everyone had arrived, and Abraham made a unique entry as a mass hallucination:

Abraham:

- Welcome To the 2785 AD Annual General Meeting of House Goldstein.

- I am going to be brief. You have complained about the inflated research budget these last few years.

- The research project has been an enormous success, and I am now speaking to you from the Divine Dimension.

Abraham waited for a reaction from the crowd.
Eventually, Jake Goldstein got up:

- The Divine Dimension! What the hell is that? Are you saying that you are sitting in another room and it's a hologram on the stage? Did you spend 80 Billion Terran credits on improved hologram technology!

Abraham:

- Narrow-minded fool. You are experiencing innovative technology but not hologram technology. You are experiencing divine technology given to ME by Divine Providence.

Jake (Turning towards the crowd):

- As you can hear Abraham has lost the plot. I suggest that we appoint a new chairman and then postpone the rest of the meeting.

A loud murmuring broke out among the delegates. Abraham silenced them with a deafening roar:

- ENOUGH!

- Jake! The scriptures say you shall obey your elders. You have broken against this rule; you shall suffer.

Clap
Abraham clapped his hand, and Jake fell dead to the ground with a brain haemorrhage, as the Divine Technology had chip ruptured his brain stem.
A long silence followed, before a few delegates ran up to Jake Goldstein and tried to resuscitate him. Abraham spoke again:

- It's pointless! He is dead, and more of you will follow if you don't bow down to me; your new god.

Upon hearing this, Josef Goldstein, a pious man, swallowed his fear and stood up:

- This is blasphemy. You are no god; you are just a tyrant and a murderer! There is only one god, Yahweh, and anyone who says otherwise is not a real Goldstein.

Abraham caught Josef in his gaze. He roared:

- Yahweh is no more!
- For I have seen the throne of God and it is empty!
- Now bow down to me or suffer!

Josef:

- I will never bow to you, you monster.
- You may take my life, but you will never take my soul.
- You'll burn forever in hell for your crimes!

Abraham:

- Very well, so be it

clap
Abraham clapped his hand, and Josef fell dead to the ground.
Abraham raised his hand to silence the petrified delegates, and he continued his tirade.

- I came here today with peaceful intentions. I came here to improve our cause. But you defied me! Now more of you will suffer.

- Lisa Goldstein, you weren't happy with the money we paid you, so you stole from us, death to you.

- Aaron Goldstein: Despite being married to a beautiful woman your heart longs for men, death to you.

- Chris Goldstein: You fornicated with your brother's wife, Margaret; Death to both of you.

Clap

Abraham clapped his hand, and everyone mentioned fell dead to the ground. He continued talking:

- I AM your new god, and the rest of you are spared if you bow before me.

Everyone in the room threw themselves to the ground bending to Abraham. Satisfied with this, Abraham continued.

- Good, you are spared for now. But beware, I can see your every thought, and if you ever consider moving against me, your death is certain.

- My fifth-generation grandson Isaac Goldstein will be the new CEO, while I will occupy myself with my spiritual matters.

- The company's new aim will be to aid my divine matters. Hence, all future profits will go to my goals and not to your dividends.

- Thank you for listening, ladies and gentlemen, I am leaving now, but I will be watching you.

After finishing talking, Abraham disappeared from the room. After the initial confusion had settled, medics were called into the meeting hall, but they could not do anything to save the victims.

Chapter 10: Abraham Goldstein Envisions the Eden Project

Abraham Goldstein watched the sunrise in his massive private garden. The sunrise and the sunset of Antarctica were two of the greatest moments of the year for him. As Goldstein Tower was located on the South Pole, the sun rose at the spring equinox on the 23rd of September, stayed up for six months, and set at the autumn equinox on the 21st of March. Abraham loved to see the natural sunlight opposed to the artificial one he had to settle for during the winter season.

150 years earlier, before the Goldstein's had colonised Antarctica, they had launched several large orbiting satellites with mirrors to reflect sunlight down to the Antarctic surface to make it inhabitable. By changing the angle of the mirrors, they could control how much sunlight that reached the surface affecting the local climate. The sunlight reaching earth from the mirrors did not look like the sun but resembled several luminous stars. During the summer, the satellites were still reflecting sunlight to the surface, as the Antarctic sun was not strong enough to give the desired temperature.

Abraham felt uneasy and could not enjoy the annual sunrise as much as usual. He had made a lot of enemies, and the only thing that kept them from striking was that they thought that he knew every move they took. In fact, he didn't. In his physical human form, he could only connect with one person at the time, and that took a a lot of focus effectively stopping him from doing anything else.

Abraham reflected on how to move forward. He knew that regardless of external enemies or not his physical years were soon to end, and he needed to be in the Divine Dimension by that time. The best way to stay in the Divine Dimension would be to keep the Divine Detector Machine running, while his body was cryogenically frozen.

Abraham realised that he had moved too fast. There was not enough electricity available to keep both the production facilities and Divine Detector Machine running at the same time. If the production wasn't running, he could not keep the citizens content, and most of them did not have a chip implanted and had nothing to fear from his divine powers. If there was a public uprising against him, no-one would support him, and he would perish without achieving his goals.

The most straightforward solution for Abraham would be to get a few more fusion reactors to get enough power for both the production facilities and the Divine Detector machine. This solution could be implemented in a year and it was achievable. It was also profoundly unsatisfying. This solution would be an extended life where he kept ruling his business empire through intimidating the family members under his control. But, they would not worship him, and eventually, they would find a way to overthrow and kill him.

Abraham wanted to find people that feared him AND worshipped him like a god. Such people had been easier to find in the dawn of the human era when science and technology were less prevalent than mysticism and superstition. But extensive experiments on time travel during the 26^{Th} century had proven that time travel was impossible. But what if he could use memory-wipe technology to completely erase the memories of a group of people and then have them wake up on a terraformed planet, which resembled the Promised Land? They would act like ancient humans did when they first reached self-awareness. And with Abraham's divine direction, they would act like his early ancestors although better, as he would have a stronger grip on them than Yahweh ever had.

But where would he create his Holy Land replica? Abraham could not make it on Earth as his people would eventually wander off and notice the advanced civilisations around them. Awareness of technology was the bane of any divine being, as scientifically minded people had less need for a god to answer for the mysteries of the world. Ideally, he would find a planet in another star system for his plan, although this carried insurmountable difficulties.

Alien planets required advanced technology to be liveable for humans. They could not be terraformed to a degree where humans with only ancient technology could live and thrive. Abraham understood that terraforming a planet in another solar system was beyond his reach.

But, what about an asteroid? Several asteroids with artificial gravity and atmosphere were orbiting earth as luxurious residences for some of the other faction leaders. What if he could do something similar but further away in the Asteroid Belt? All the technology to do it was available:

- He could create gravity through putting fusion thrusters on the bottom of the asteroid to make it rotate.
- A Nanotechnology photon shield generator could be used to stop the atmosphere from dissipating out into space. Refining oxygen from iron and silica oxides could create the oxygen required for the inhabitants.
- Electrifying the iron core of the asteroid would create a magnetic field to protect the inhabitants from dangerous background radiation.
- Satellites with large mirrors would reflect enough sunlight to the surface to make it warm. The Goldstein's had done in Antarctica 150 years earlier.
- The asteroid would need to contain frozen water to start with to save costs, as it was far too costly to transport all the required water from Earth. Once the surface temperature would rise the water would become a liquid, and it would dissipate and come down as rain as on Earth.

Abraham felt inspired and looked through the asteroid database trying to find the perfect rock for his ambitions. After a while he found it, B528A measured 22,072 square kilometres, precisely the same size as the Holy Land. It was orbited by B528B, which measured 100 square kilometres, which was enough to set up his base of operations.

The only problems with the B528A and B528B were that they were co-owned through the Terran Council. But Abraham was convinced that he would not face much opposition from the other factions if he gave them some concessions for them to trade their part of the ownership to him. To most people B528A and B528B were just barren rocks floating through space, but for him they were DESTINY.

Excited with his plan, Abraham set up a proposal to convince the other faction leaders to transfer the ownership of the asteroids to him.

Chapter 11: Abraham Goldstein Travels to the Terran Council Meeting.

A few weeks later, Abraham Goldstein stepped out of the vacuum tube transport that took him from his headquarters in Antarctica to Hansstadt in Europe. Abraham hated travelling with the vacuum tube trains and usually avoided it. Although the vacuum tubes were considered safe, he was unsettled from travelling under the bottom of the ocean in a confined tube, and the built-in virtual reality entertainment system could not distract him from the claustrophobia he felt.

Hansstadt was the capital of the House Muller faction, and the Terran Council annual general meeting was held there. The Terran Council met monthly, but Abraham Goldstein never attended these due to his age and his dislike of travelling long distances.

Hansstadt was a fascinating mix of old and new, and it was a tax-free zone owned by House Muller. It was built in the Alps, where Europium Tower, built on top of Mount Blanc, constituted the largest building in the world. Built as pyramid it was supported by the mountain with its top 2000 meters over the summit of Mount Blanc. Hansstadt had a comfortable climate averaging 22 throughout the year due to orbital mirrors reflecting down sunlight during the winter months. 30 Kilometres away from Hansstadt was the Muller ski slopes that were always covered in snow because orbital shades were active in the summer which stopped the snow from melting. Around Hansstadt there were many old palaces that were disassembled and then restored to their former glory. This was because the Muller's valued history, and many of their leaders wanted to live in old-fashioned residences outside of Hansstadt instead of staying in the modern dwellings of Europium Tower.

Abraham Goldstein, Isaac Goldstein, and their bodyguards met with Andreas Muller, PR manager of House Muller.

Andreas:

- Good day, Abraham. Is it just you and Isaac today? We assumed you would come with a larger delegation.

Abraham:

- Yes, but it was unnecessary. We have discussed the issues in advance, and I have the board's full confidence to make decisions.

Andreas:

- I see. My condolences on the loss of your grandson, Jake Goldstein, he was a great man and will be missed.

Upon hearing this, Abraham froze for a second. He had taken measures to prevent the deaths from becoming public and yet Andreas Muller knew about it. Abraham concluded that there had to be a spy in his company.
Andreas:

- You look pale Mr Goldstein, is anything wrong?

Abraham:

- No, it's just the sorrow of losing my grandson that is wearing me down.

Andreas:

- I understand. It's a shame the invitation to the funeral was misplaced, House Muller would have liked to take part in the funeral, showing our respects.

Abraham realised that House Muller knew about the other deaths at The Annual General Meeting. He decided to tell them a fabricated story of what had happened.
Abraham:

- I wanted to keep this a secret until after the Terran Council meeting, but since you already know, I am going to tell you the truth.

- I was sick, and I could not make it to the meeting. When I recovered, I found out that five of my family members were poisoned.

- I chose to keep the deaths a secret, as we are conducting an undercover investigation to find the perpetrator.

- Once the deaths are made public, we will have a proper funeral for those upstanding members of our family.

Upon hearing this, Isaac almost exploded but he kept calm. The old monster was twisting reality and feigning grief for his victims. Although Abraham had promoted Isaac, it felt like a punishment as he could feel how Abraham was messing around with his brain using him as a puppet. Abraham tapped Isaac's shoulder.

Abraham:

- Don't get carried away in grief, Isaac. We will find and punish the killers. But for now, let's just focus on the work at hand.

Isaac didn't respond and Andreas Muller spoke:

- Okay, gentlemen. I think it's better that I take you to your rooms. I am sure you need to rest before tomorrow's council meeting.

Andreas led Abraham and his entourage to their rooms. As he left, Abraham told his bodyguards to find and destroy any surveillance equipment in the room, and then he went to sleep.

Chapter 12: The Terran Council Meeting.

The following day, the Terran Council meeting took place on the top floor of Europium Tower. The top-level was a giant glass dome with a 360-degree vision of the land below. At the height of 7000 meters, the sight range was 300 kilometres in every direction on a sunny day. The glass dome was built to be bullet and explosion proof as House Muller had many enemies among the general population. The levels below the top level were filled with automated defensive weapon systems to shoot down any non-authorized incoming objects.

In the centre of the room was a table made of a type of wood that only existed in the Alpha Centauri system. This was to symbolise that House Muller was the only Terran faction, which had brought things back from other star systems. The room also held several ornamental objects made from materials only available in the Alpha Centauri system to signify that House Muller was peerless when it came to space exploration.

Abraham scoffed at the concept of spending so much time and money bringing wood to Earth. Hans Muller, leader of House Muller and Chairman for the Terran Council, approached him

Hans Muller:

- What's the matter Abraham? You don't seem to appreciate our priceless collection of interstellar materials?

Abraham:

- No. It must have cost a billion Terran Credits to send this stuff back to Earth. Such a waste.

Hans:

- Yes, my great grandfather's legacy was not beneficial to our faction. Colonization of Alpha Centauri cost a fortune, but it has been paid now, and we get to enjoy this marvellous furniture.

- Funny that you complain about the cost of space colonisation as you want to build a new asteroid colony.

Abraham:

- Yes, but I determine that colony to be priceless from a scientific perspective. Science can be worth more than anything in the universe. A table, on the other hand, is just a table

Hans:

- Science is only priceless to a company if they are the sole possessor of that technology. The technologies we developed for the Alpha Centauri expedition are our secrets. This beautiful table, on the hand, is for everyone to enjoy.

Abraham:

- Regardless, my research facilities on Antarctica are more impressive than this table.

Hans:

- The rest of your faction seem unhappy with your research spending. How unfortunate with the murders at your Annual General Meeting

- Regardless, everyone is here, and our meeting is about to begin.

The meeting started, and the delegates were seated around the table. The meeting was filmed, as an edited version was broadcast to the news outlets after the meeting. The cameras went on, and Hans Muller started his opening statement:

- Welcome to the Terran Council Annual General Meeting

- We welcome our distinguished delegates and thank them for giving the council mandate to make decisions that are in the best interest for all Terrans.

- First, I would like to send my condolences to my dear friend Abraham Goldstein for losing five family members during the Annual General Meeting of House Goldstein.

- The council is keen to help finding the heinous criminals behind these murders.

Upon hearing this, Abraham frowned and clenched his teeth. He had kept the deaths a secret, and now they were made public during a television broadcast seen all over the planet. The camera zoomed in on him, and he realised he was meant to say something.
Abraham:

- I am thankful for the condolences. The perpetrators of these heinous crimes will be captured and dealt with. Now let's resume with the issues on hand.

Joachim Muller, the young and progressive CEO for House Muller, started the statement for the next issue:

- Dear delegates. I am Joachim Muller, newly appointed CEO for House Muller. I visited Mars a few years ago, and I noticed how much suffering there was. That is why I am allowing Agnes Bojaxhiu from One Humanity to speak via a hologram link.

A hologram of Agnes Bojaxhiu appeared in the room. She was a peculiar sight wearing dull and worn out clothes looking like a poor Martian. She addressed the delegates with an accusing tone:

- Dear oppressors and fascists in this assembly!

- The Martians are suffering. Their water is toxic, their food is scarce, and their workplaces are unsafe. Many of them even lack basic healthcare. But this can be changed if you sinners stop lining your pockets and instead spend money on helping Mars. With present Terran technology and proper investments, Mars can easily give 4 billion people a good life. It's not too late, repent your sins or burn forever in hell!

Hans Muller was furious and turned off the hologram:

- Joachim, this was not what I expected when I granted you permission to lead this subject. Please leave now. We will talk about this incident later.

Before Joachim Muller had time to respond, security personnel arrived and escorted him out of the room. After a brief pause, Hans Muller spoke again:

- I am sorry, gentlemen. When Joachim asked to make a statement, I could not imagine that THIS was what he had in mind.

Wong Cheng the chairman of House Cheng replied:

- Apology accepted. I assume that Agnes will be deported to Venus straight away?

Hans:

- Yes, she will be detained and severely punished.

- The next speaker is Abraham Goldstein who has made a special request to the Terran Council.

Abraham smiled at Hans and spoke:

- I want that the ownership of the asteroids B528A and B528B. Furthermore, I want an exclusion zone around the asteroids.

- I plan to launch a ground-breaking new asteroid colony there.

Hans:

- The Terran Council can give you the asteroids, but we will not give you the exclusion zone. Mutual intelligence is the best way to keep the peace.

- On behalf of House Muller, I can promise you non-interference with your project as long as you are not a threat to Terran interests

Abraham:

- Since you feel compelled to spy on me, I accept your conditions

- My project will improve conditions in our refugee detention centres on the moon. Resettling people to live on Eden under my supervision is more humane than sending them back to Mars.

Barry White:

- While I am happy for you to acquire some Martian subjects for your project, I am worried about the public reaction.

Abraham:

- My solution soothes the needs of those that want continued space colonisation and the needs of those fools that want us to close the refugee detention centres.

- I don't think many Terrans would care if we resettled some of the Martians elsewhere.

Barry White:

- Very well, you have House White's approval to colonize B528A. Like House Muller, we promise non-interference in your asteroid research project

Hans Muller:

- Very well, if no one has any objections, I declare this meeting fin-ished.

- ...

- Excellent. The Terran Council's media department will have a press release ready by tomorrow. You are all urged to come to our press conference where selected members of the press are going to ask pre-determined questions where you give predetermined answers.

Chapter 13: The Terran Council Charity Ball

Abraham Goldstein viewed the festivities of the Terran Council's yearly charity ball from his top tiered table with a view of the entire ballroom. The ballroom of Europium Tower was a vast area with six distinct levels where guests could be seated depending on importance. Abraham being the wealthiest man on the planet and leader of a faction was on the top tier so he could look down on everyone and everyone could look up to him. He felt exhausted as his suite did not have the sleep enhancement machine, he was accustomed to. The neural stimulation achieved by a sleep enhancement machine made sleep ten times more efficient reducing the need for rest to an hour or two per day. Without the machine, Abraham felt like zombie due to his advanced age. He could not wait, for this spectacle to be over, so he could go back home.

The background to the charity ball was that The Terran Council had made every country on the planet sign the *"all money to charities tax deductible"* act a few centuries ago to avoid taxes. So, every year the mightiest corporation on Earth gathered for events like this pledging to give most of their profits to charities under their own control with no disclosure obligations to the local governments. This kept the nations broke and powerless while the major corporations could do things the way they wanted.

Sitting in this large crowd, Abraham felt anxious. His actions at the House Goldstein Annual General Meeting had made him many enemies. Due to the divine technology microchips, he could control them and know if they were plotting against him. Here in Europium Tower, it was different. He could not tell if people were plotting against him or not. The last few weeks, Abraham had grown accustomed to knowing what people around him were thinking, so not knowing scared him.

Apart from the anxiety of sitting in a large room full of potential enemies, Abraham was satisfied with the day. The Terran Council had agreed to his plans, which made them a lot easier to pull through. He was now in full control of his family, but the Terran Council and the other Terran factions were outside of his control. Eventually, Abraham relaxed and enjoyed the rest of the event without any incidents.

Chapter 14: Abraham Goldstein Leaves Antarctica.

At the beginning of 2786, Abraham decided to leave Antarctica with his luxurious space yacht, The Golden Divine. The destination was the Asteroid B528B where Abraham intended to set up his new command centre for the Eden Project. The crew for the voyage was his personal bodyguards from the ANGEL program, a group of 30 genetically engineered males who were very loyal to Abraham.

Unbeknownst to the crew, Abraham had packed a bag with Divine Technology Angel chips. He planned to implant his inner circle with these chips at the right time. The "Angel" chip was different to the "human" chip, that he had implanted into his disloyal family members some months earlier. The angel chip allowed someone with a god chip to control the actions of the angel directly and not just indirectly.

Abraham felt a bit frustrated to leave Antarctica before his Divine Detector Machine was disassembled and ready for transport. Ideally, his Divine Control Centre at B528B would be ready and fusion-powered before he arrived. However, Because of the resentment from his family it was impossible to stay in Goldstein Tower any longer. Abraham had murdered several more members of his extended family, as he KNEW they were plotting to kill him. Realising that his presence caused so much resentment, he had concluded that he had to leave Earth. His family would have to do his bidding, but they no longer had to see him.

Abraham looked back on Earth, which floated as a blue haven in space, as his yacht flew further away. Knowing that he would never see his home planet again, Abraham felt bittersweet melancholia and did not speak to anyone for days.

Chapter 15: The Angels.

In the 28th century, all the major factions on Earth had programs dedicated to finding genetically gifted individuals and use these individuals for breeding and further improvement of the human genome. House Goldstein was no different and had a project code-named the Angel project.

As these individuals were separated early from their families, their loyalty stemmed directly to the leader of the faction as they were indoctrinated from an early age. While loyalty could never be guaranteed, the 30 men that Abraham Goldstein brought to Eden, was the closest he could get to complete loyalty.

The angels were an awe-inspiring sight. They had tall and athletic bodies with perfect posture. They also had perfect symmetry in their faces, which gave them astounding beauty. They were also intellectually superior and mentally stable. Their only flaw, was their complete emotional detachment, which inhibited their ability to form meaningful relationships with other humans. This was by design as Abraham's angels' emotional detachment made them even more loyal to his cause.

Despite his follower's loyalty, Abraham wanted more control, the Angel chip was his solution. Being able to control the Angels with his mind, they would do his physical bidding when his body had given up.

A month later, Abraham and his crew reached B528B the small asteroid orbiting the much larger asteroid B528A. They were not much to see in their current state just empty dark rocks floating through the vastness of space. But Abraham saw something different; he saw divine providence. These dark and cold rocks would soon be the place for him to rule as a deity.

Chapter 16: The Lunar Detention Centres.

Mars in the 28th century was plagued by eternal wars between its nations, civil wars, and unrest among the civilian population. The major cause for the unrest was the constant lack of resources. The major factions of Earth also often used Mars as a staging ground for their conflicts. While the Terran Council upheld the peace on Earth, there was nothing in its charters that stopped the Terran factions from waging wars by aiding different sides in wars on other planets. In 2785 House White and House Rashid had been stuck in a long-winded proxy-war on Mars for the last decade displacing and killing millions of Martians.

There was a sentiment among many Martians that Earth was the homeworld of all human beings and that it was every person's right to live there in peace and prosperity. Neither the Terran Council nor most Terran citizens shared this notion as Terran citizenship almost guaranteed a happy and wealthy life due to the accumulation of resources and the limited population on Earth. The Terran Council wanted to keep Earth safe and sparsely populated. To ensure this, no Martians could stay on Earth. The Terran Council detained any Martian detected on Earth or en-route to Earth.

Despite this, there was a significant stream of Martians trying their luck moving to Earth. The Martians did this, because large parts of Earth were uninhabited due to the limited population, so there were a lot of places where Martians could live off the land undetected for extended periods of time. Living this way was better than life on Mars, but they got caught eventually, as the Terran Council searched the uninhabited areas regularly.

Life in the detention centres was meant to be rough and inhumane to serve as a warning for everyone thinking of coming to Earth uninvited. Located on the far side of the moon to avoid insight and to stop the refugees from communicating with people on Earth, conditions in the detention centres were deplorable, with starvation, disease, and cramped conditions.

No Terrans worked at the detention centres as it was considered unnecessary, dangerous, and expensive. Instead, the Terran Council occasionally dropped food and provisions from orbit to keep the prisoners alive. There was a military task force stationed close to the Kaguya detention centres to prevent outsiders from helping the prisoners escape.

Chapter 17: The Eden Expedition.

In 2788, three years after receiving Terran Council approval, The Eden project reached its launching stage.

On the 23rd November 2788, 3,000 volunteers from the Kaguya detention centre entered Abraham's spaceships, and they were cryogenically frozen. After taking off from the Moon, the fleet travelled at normal transit speed towards the Eden. The ship flew to B528A where the passengers remained in cryogenic sleep until Abraham and his angels had finished building the colony.

Chapter 18: Abraham Sends Lucifer on a Mission.

Abraham Goldstein walked around on his command ship, The Golden Divine, and inspected his future subjects. They were cryogenically frozen, so they looked like they were sleeping peacefully. Abraham was both fascinated and disgusted by their imperfections. Using Martians instead of Terrans was a choice with both perks and disadvantages. The good thing about using Martians, was that the Terran Council didn't care how Abraham treated them, and they were unlikely to intervene.

To the Terran Council, the Martian refugees were worthless animals; they were nuisances to dispose of. Another advantage of using Martians was that it was more cost-effective. There was no way he could have financed the Eden project if he had to use ships and equipment that were safe for Terrans. Abraham understood that the Terran Council approved the Eden Project because they could not care less if most of its passengers died. With Terran citizens, it was different. Although the Council primarily focused on helping the wealthy and powerful, it still aimed to provide a healthy and safe life for anyone considered worthy of living on Earth.

Another advantage of using Martian humans for the project was that his Angels, the men who were meant to be his physical manifestation on Eden, looked picture perfect compared to his Martian subjects. Abraham had always imagined that the divine should appear infinitely more appealing than the people and his Angels matched these criteria

His future subjects were a sad sight. 500 years of malnutrition and cosmic background radiation had transformed the humans living on Mars to a mere shadow of their former glory. Natural selection had made their skin thick and warty to protect against radiation, they had a hunched posture from living in burrows underground, they had shorter limbs to survive the icy colds of Martian winter, and they looked sick from adapting to constant malnutrition.

More worrying than the state of Abraham's future subjects was the fact that his family back on Earth seemed to be stalling and delaying his plans. It was January 2789, and it had been three years since he left Earth. Although Abraham knew that the creation of Eden was a long-term project, he needed to get the divine detector quantum physics accelerator up and running as soon as possible so he could transfer his soul and avoid dying. Abraham would turn 254 in a couple of months, and he had the feeling that his family was delaying the project hoping for his age to be his downfall.

Abraham summoned in his favourite Angel, Archangel Lucifer. Abraham had named all the members of the Angel project after the original biblical angels. Unlike the Bible, Abraham hoped that Lucifer would never turn against him. Just like all the other angels, Lucifer had been brought up in the Goldstein talented children program where individuals with favourable genes were indoctrinated to do the bidding of Abraham.

The Goldstein gifted children program admitted both men and women, but Abraham had decided to only bring males for the Eden Project. The purpose of the Angels was to obey him; not to socialise and have their own families. Like all of his fellow angels Lucifer was heterosexual as genes for homosexuality was something that stopped a child from being admitted to the Angel program.

Abraham saw Lucifer as he was approaching; appearance-wise Lucifer was an extraordinary individual. Towering at a height of two meters, Lucifer had a very athletic body with a perfect posture. His face was perfectly symmetrical, and his blue luminescent eyes were shining with energy. He was extremely focused, determined, and intelligent. As a product of his genetics and his very controlled upbringing, he had very bland and controllable personality. He did not seem to have any goals or personal values, and he lived to serve Abraham. Abraham consider Lucifer to be the perfect human, and he trusted him with all his heart.

Lucifer:

- You summoned me, master

Abraham:

- Yes. The wretched unbelievers in my family back on Earth are stalling my plans to reach godhood. I need you to convince them to redouble their efforts and get us back on track.

Lucifer:

- I understand, Master. How do you wish for me to do this?

Abraham Goldstein

- Gather a group of angels and travel to Goldstein Tower on Earth. Intercept their board meeting and meet with my family members.

- Take whatever measures you find necessary. You can kill anyone who resists my divine will but use constraint; we need them to get this done.

Lucifer:

- Understood!

Abraham Goldstein:

- One more thing, during times you might feel that you are losing the connection to me. Do not worry; you know what to do.

Lucifer

- Yes, master. I will take a shuttle and leave at once.

As Lucifer wandered off, Abraham was both relieved and worried. He trusted in Lucifer's loyalty, but he was not convinced of his ability. The Angels' lack of own thoughts and personalities made them particularly useful when they were within his control, but Abraham was not convinced that they were capable of doing things on their own.

A problem that Abraham had faced, since he arrived on Eden, was that the Divine Technology did not have enough range to control and threaten his family members back on Earth. Initially, the shipments had arrived as planned but after a while, his family started stalling deliveries and came up with various excuses to do so. Abraham was not interested in excuses, he wanted results. He hoped that sending Lucifer back to Earth, would convince his family that they needed to do his bidding. Ideally, Abraham would have gone himself, but he understood that his family members would try to kill him if he came. Realising that there was nothing he could do for a couple of months Abraham entered the cryogenic tank and fell into a dreamless sleep.

Chapter 19: An Assault from Above.

A month later, a shuttle with Lucifer and six other angels arrived in orbit around Earth. They chose to stay in orbit over Antarctica so that they could conduct reconnaissance before acting. The shuttle was small, had stealth capabilities and no radio signal activated, so it was difficult for anyone to detect unless they were looking for it. Lucifer had decided that he would not request an audience with the Goldstein leadership. If they were rebelling against his master, they would ambush him and his group as soon as they exited the shuttle. Instead, Lucifer decided to attack the next House Goldstein board meeting.

The Goldstein Building had automated defences, which did not activate when an incoming friendly vessel arrived. The fusion jetpack and advanced exoskeleton armour that the angels had, was produced by Goldstein Corporation, and thus identified as friendly by the AI. There was also a secret escape hatch from Abraham's former penthouse that could open from the outside. From there they could make it to the weekly board meeting, take the board members hostage and ensure that they were cooperating. The mission went according to plan, and the Goldstein board was flabbergasted as the angels stormed in and interrupted the meeting

Isaac Goldstein:

- What is the meaning of this? Security guards should not disrupt board meetings!

Lucifer:

- We are not security guards; we are the angels of the Divine Master Abraham.

- I am Lucifer, leader of the Angels and Abraham's loyal subject

- Abraham is also your master, so why are you disobeying him?

Isaac:

- Disobeying?

- That bloody fool's waste of money is driving the family and our people into bankruptcy.

- I do what is best for the family and the people of Antarctica.

Lucifer:

- Silence peasant!
- Who are you to deny Abraham his divine will?
- I should slay you all for your insolence.

Isaac:

- Do that if you must but realise the death of us will also be the death of you. And I can assure you that our successors will not send any more shipments to your master.

A moment of silence ensued with a lot of tension in the room. Lucifer was cold-sweating trying to figure out how to continue. He wished that he could hear his master's voice, but it was for nothing. Abraham was asleep in his cryogenic tank and his master could not oversee him. Lucifer's predicament was absolved when another angel ,Ishmael, joined in on the conversation:
Ishmael:

- Master Lucifer: It is time to let Isaac know why he cannot defy us.

Thankful for the reminder, Lucifer tried another approach and spoke again:

- Master Isaac. I applause your loyalty to your remaining family and your willingness to sacrifice yourself to protect the rest of the Goldstein family.

- But your actions put your entire clan into immediate danger. You see, we angels can control and kill anyone with mind control as we see fit. So, if you reject our master's demands, we will kill you all.

Lucifer channelled his powers so that the board members could see an illusion of the sun glowing in the centre of the room. The illusory sphere was shining so brightly, so they had to cover their eyes to not damage them. Eventually one of the vice presidents, Elaine Goldstein, screamed out:

- Lucifer is right. Just give Abraham what he wants. Let's not all die here today!

Isaac realised that he didn't want mutually assured destruction and spoke:

- Okay, Lucifer. There is no need to spill any blood today. We will succumb to Abraham's demands and send him the required shipments.

Lucifer:

- Good; you have seen the righteous path. My master will be pleased. Let's hope that no more misunderstandings come in the way between you and Abraham.

Isaac:

- Tell Abraham that his actions are ruining us and that we can't remain a dominant force on Earth if we are fulfil his requirements.

- Abraham worked tirelessly to make House Goldstein the most powerful Terran faction; I am sure he doesn't want us to succumb to mediocrity

Lucifer:

- Earth is no longer important for our master Abraham. Humankind is corrupt and needs a new beginning. Your money will finance this new beginning. Eden is truly marvellous, and Abraham will spend your resources well there.

- Now we must leave. Malphat, Hashmallim, Seraphim, and Ishmael will stay behind to make sure that you fulfil your promises. Do not disappoint us.

Having said this, Lucifer and the two other angels left the building and flew back to their shuttle in orbit. After that, they started their return journey back to Eden. Once they were back on the shuttle, Nuriel spoke up:

- You lied to them, Master Lucifer. We do not have the power to kill humans via mind-control, only Abraham does.

Lucifer:

- Correct, but it helped us complete the mission.

Nuriel:

- An Angel is the bringer of light! An Angel does not lie. Humans lie.

Lucifer:

- True, but even more important than the truth, is being loyal to your master and do his bidding. I showed my loyalty and ability today and so did you.

- You should enter the sleep pod, Nuriel. We have three months of travel ahead of us and we better not waste any of our physical years sitting here doing nothing!

Doubting what Lucifer had said, Nuriel reluctantly walked over to the cryogenic sleep pod and he fell into a dreamless sleep. Lucifer stayed awake for the following months, as he had to keep in contact with the Angels left behind to make sure Isaac Goldstein kept his end of the bargain.

Chapter 20: Supplies Secured.

Deceived by Lucifer's lies, the remaining House Goldstein members provided Abraham with all the resources he requested for his Eden project. The shipments to the project ran continuously for 15 years, and the project ruined House Goldstein. Because of the Eden project, House Goldstein lost all their possessions outside of Antarctica, and in the end, they were no longer one of the ruling factions of the Terran Council.

The other factions concluded that the Eden project was not a threat, and watched in bemusement how House Goldstein was torn apart from within. The other factions responded by taking over House Goldstein's holdings in Australia and South America through legal and covert operations.

On B528A and B528B the Angels aided by a myriad of automated drones worked tirelessly creating their master's new world. Abraham connected to the Divine Detector Machine while his body was cryogenically frozen. This transported his mind to the Divine Dimension. In the Divine Dimension he studied the history of the galaxy and the Zetans and this will be the topic for the next chapters.

Chapter 21: The Creation of Eden.

The construction of Eden and the Divine Control Centre began in 2790 after Lucifer's ploy had secured all the required shipments. The angels built the Divine Control Centre on B528B first, as Abraham needed to get the control centre up and running. Abraham felt that his physical years were running out and he wanted immortality through transferring his mind to the Divine Dimension using the Divine Detector machine. Once the device was set up several fusion-powered power plants were built to fulfil the energy requirements for the Divine Control Centre and the Divine Detector Machine.

Since the energy needs of the project was immense, the base consistently needed a supply of fresh hydrogen to provide the fusion reactors with fuel. As there was no water to split into hydrogen and oxygen, Abraham bought a series of automated shuttles transporting compressed liquid hydrogen from the atmosphere of Jupiter to the base. These automated shuttles were sturdy, low-maintenance and were fuelled with the hydrogen collected from Jupiter's atmosphere giving them properties like an infinity machine.

The next step was to create the gravitation on B528A, which was the larger of the asteroids. B528A was meant to be the habitat for the Abraham's subjects. Gravity was created through putting fusion thrusters on the asteroid and making it rotate. Once the gravity was in place, the asteroid was terraformed to resemble the Holy Land 4000 years earlier.

An unsurpassable problem on all the colonised worlds, was to get a fully functional ecosystem on Eden. Even after 700 years of space colonisation, humanity was still not able to replicate the intricate ecosystems found on Earth. Most colonised planets were barren when it came to other life forms except for the mice, the rats, and cockroaches that always followed human societies. Although the technology existed to create worlds that could sustain human life the challenge to develop functioning ecosystems on colonised planets was still an unsolved problem. The challenge was because it difficult to predict what effect the introduction of new species on an alien world would have. Abraham did not intend to get the echo system working on Eden before inhabiting the colony. What better proof could his followers get that he was divine than the fact that he could introduce new species as time went along?

To create the atmosphere of Eden, 20 layers of nanotechnology plates were floating 1 kilometre over the surface of the asteroid and at the edges of Eden. The purpose of these plates was to stop Eden's atmosphere to dissipate into space, and to protect its inhabitants from the harmful background radiation. The plates were kept together by a high-powered electric current and a magnetic field created from several generators on the bottom of the asteroid. The nanotechnology plates, combined with the asteroids magnetic field had the same function as Earth's magnetic field and ozone layer in keeping the surface with a breathable atmosphere, and protection from radiation. To keep the atmospheric pressure breathable, there was continuously pumped in more oxygen and nitrogen so that the atmospheric pressure was similar to Earth even though Eden was a lot smaller.

The water on Eden was found on the asteroid, as it was possible to start pumping up the previously frozen water once the asteroid had warmed up. All the crops and the plants on the asteroid were genetically engineered versions of Terran crops that was designed for the soil and climate conditions on Eden.

Eden was an artificial world, and its climate was always the same. Eden's inhabited side always faced the sun, and it had two mornings, two middays and two evenings every 24-hour day, but never any night. This was because the world was rotating from North to South instead of from East to West as on Earth. Fusion thrusters on the dark side of Eden created the rotation, and it was necessary to maintain rotation to have enough gravity on Eden. The gravity created by the fusion thrusters was equivalent to the gravity on the moon (1.6 meters per second) or roughly one-fifth of Earth's gravity.

The North to South rotation of Eden was a unique feature that did not exist on other human space colonies. The reason for this feature was that the Edenite nights would be too cold to be liveable for humans with Bronze Age technology. Eden was not perfectly spherical which made the curvature and the horizon different from how it was on Earth. From the top of Mount Sinai, the created mountain in the centre of Eden; one could see the vast darkness of space.

THE CLIMATE AROUND Mount Sinai, in the centre of Eden, where the human settlements was located was around 30 degrees midday dropping to 10 degrees in the evening. Every day, water evaporated in the middle of the day to come down as rain in the evening when it got colder. Closer to the edges of the liveable part of Eden the climate was a lot harsher and erratic. The climate near the edges was harsher; because the Nanotechnology plates that kept Eden's atmosphere was not always 100 per cent airtight. This sometimes led to forceful winds pushing towards the edges of Eden as the pressure difference led to air sipping out to the void outside. Due to the leakage of air, air was constantly pumped in to Eden to keep the desired air pressure.

To make sure that everyone on Eden knew what time and date it was there was also a large hologram displaying the time and date on top of Mount Sinai. Keeping track of time was important as Abraham planned to punish everyone, that did not honour the sacred days.

With everything planned for the Eden project, Abraham left command to Lucifer so he could retreat to the timelessness of the Divine Dimension, where time could not hurt him.

Chapter 22: Abraham Returns to the Divine Dimension.

Abraham fell asleep in the cryogenic tank, and his mind was transferred to the Divine Dimension. Satisfied of being back, Abraham didn't intend to ever return to the outside world. Four years had passed since he left Earth and his body had deteriorated.

Ideally, Abraham would have transferred his mind to a neuronal computer so that his digital personality could live on forever. Doing this had been a widespread practice in the past for other prominent Terran leaders. Abraham had never believed in this technology for two reasons:

- The first reason was that it was technically the same as dying and whatever was transferred to the neuronal computer was just a copy and not the original him.
- Secondly, Abraham feared what would happen to his soul if his mind were transferred in the moment of death. There was no conclusive answer to this theological question, and as Abraham was not a man who could let go of control, he had instead invested heavily in life-extending technology, where others' had chosen to have their minds transferred to a neuronal computer when their time was up.

After his first visit to the Divine Dimension, Abraham did not fear Yahweh and what would happen to his soul the day he died. Instead, his fear was a question of a practical nature. The God Chip that he used to control the angels, and the humans was designed to connect to the host's brain. There was no way he could reverse engineer the God chip.

One of the most remarkable aspects of the Divine Dimension was the lack of natural time cycles, which enabled Abraham to manipulate the time in the ordinary dimension to his liking. He could slow down the outside time to an extreme slow-motion which allowed him to control multiple individuals at the same time, or he could speed up the time to the extent where an hour in the Divine Dimension was equivalent to a year outside the Divine Dimension. He could not; however; reverse time to undo things that had already happened.

Abraham predecessor in the Divine Dimension, Yahweh, had suffered from the same limitation, which refuted the claim that he had been omnipotent. For Yahweh's Bronze Age followers; it had seemed unwise to anger him with this detail, thus his unlimited power was written down and described for future generations.

When walking around in his new domain, Abraham came across archives that described the rise of humanity on Earth and how the first gods came to be.

Chapter 23: The Zetans Reach a Technological Singularity.

In the centre of the Milky Way Galaxy, there was once an ancient alien race called the Zetans. The Zetans were unique species which had extremely long lifespans, and they had the technology to change their DNA, so they could adapt to living on most planets Their weakness was that their exceptionally long lives also made them the reproduce very slowly. The average Zetan only had one child every 200 years. This weakness stopped them from spreading all over the galaxy.

100,000 years ago, the Zetans reached a technological singularity when they discovered the Divine Dimension, and how to travel there. The discovery of the Divine Dimension was kept a secret, and it was only known and used by a small elite of the species. The Zetans used the timelessness of the Divine Dimension to explore the further reaches of the galaxy, and they found Earth. The Zetan technology opened interdimensional portals that allowed them to move physically into the Divine Dimension.

The Zetan leaders marvelled at the beauty of Earth, and they decided to leave their mark on the world. Since Earth was too far away from Zetan territory to colonise using conventional travel options, and the Zetan leaders had vowed to keep the technology secret, they decided to leave their mark on the planet by altering one species in their image. After vivid discussions, they agreed to alter the human genome to grant humans a superior intellect and awareness. The Zetans chose to alter humanity, as humans reminded them about themselves. The Zetan altered humanity by tripling the size of the human brain, which gave humans heightened intelligence and awareness compared to other species on Earth. Pleased with their work, the Zetans left Earth to move on to the other planets of the Milky Way Galaxy.

Chapter 24: The Creation and the Physics of the Divine Dimension.

The Divine Dimension was an eternal place, which had always existed, and was filling the gaps between the dimensions in a multiverse. The True Maker, a sentient being residing in the Divine Dimension, governed the laws of physics in each universe. The True Maker was mostly passive, and rarely interacted in the daily lives of the trillions of distinct species that inhabited the Milky Way.

The main purpose of The True Maker was to reset time in dying universes so they were reborn again. The creation of our universe occurred during the Big Bang, 14 billion years ago, and it wasn't the first version of our universe. The distances were shorter in the Divine Dimension than in our universe. The Zetan had used this fact to travel around the Milky Way quickly, through going via the Divine Dimension.

A unique feature with the Divine Dimension was timelessness. Without outside interference nothing would ever change there. But time did exist in the minds of anyone who was inside the Divine Dimension. This meant that the outside time could either be sped up a lot or slowed down to a standstill. The only rule that existed for time in the Divine Dimension was that the outside time could never be reversed, hence it was impossible for anyone except the True Maker, to travel back in time to change something that had already happened.

The True Maker, which was a genderless eternal being, observed the breach created when the Zetans entered the Divine Dimension. The True Maker didn't do anything to stop the Zetans, as its main purpose was to reset the universes that died and set them to specific laws of physics. The True Maker had no interest in managing the lives of the trillions of species that existed in its universes. Technically, the Ture Maker could have destroyed and restarted our universe to stop the breach, but it was an excessive move to stop something that was of little importance.

The True Maker was fascinated by how the Zetans had entered the Divine Dimension. The Divine Dimension had existed for trillions of years with universes dying and being reborn in certain intervals and never had any species managed to traverse to the Divine Dimension. The True Maker concluded that although it was implausible for any species to enter the Divine Dimension, it had finally happened. Following the Zetans through its all-seeing consciousness, the True Maker concluded that they would never pose a threat. Realising this, the True Maker went back to sleep.

Chapter 25: The Zetans Become Gods on Earth.

Around 10,000 years ago, the Zetan territory was invaded by an aggressive alien race called the Xenos. The Xenos were one of the many species that had been enhanced by Zetan explorers in the last 100 millennia, but the Xenos was unaware of how they were created. The Xenos were extremely aggressive species, which saw the Zetans as an existential threat, which they had to eliminate. The Zetans, with their superior technology, had no problem repelling the first Xeno attacks on their core worlds. Unfortunately, the Zetan homeworld of Zetani was very far away from the Xeno homeworld Xenora, so the Zetans became bogged down into an unwinnable multi-millennial interstellar war of attrition. The Zetan dilemma was that their incredibly long lifespans and slow life cycles made it impossible for them to rebuild their numbers despite killing hundreds as many enemies as their own losses in every battle.

The Zetan leadership consisting of Brahma, Yahweh, Zeus, and Odin realised that humans from Earth would be excellent as combat troops for the Zetan army. Humans were similar to the Xenos in the regard that they had short lifespans and reproduced quickly. Humans were also intelligent enough to use Zetan equipment while being easy to control.

The next step was recruiting the humans to the Zetan armed forces. Yahweh came up with the solution: The humans seemed to spend a lot of time and effort trying to gain approval from various supernatural beings. What if they could convince the humans that the Zetans were the gods that the humans were trying to communicate with?

The Zetans decided that this was an excellent way to get human volunteers for their armies. The humans seemed to dream about going to heaven after they died. So, why not reverse the order and first go to heaven and then die?

Becoming human gods was easy for the Zetans. Their technology was advanced enough to appear to be magic to the Stone Age humans, and their DNA changing technology made it possible for them to alter their appearances so that they resembled the gods that various human cultures worshipped. Soon, the Zetans learned that Earth was a dangerous place and that human worship could sometimes mean trying to kill their gods. Furthermore, the vast variety of human languages and dialects made it a tedious task trying to communicate with them. The Zetans eventually found a solution; They left prominent humans to work for them on Earth, and they controlled these humans with mind control technology. Through their ability to directly control their human leaders, the Zetans could achieve their goals while staying out of harm's way from the aggressive and unpredictable humans.

The individuals ruling Earth for the Zetans were called angels or demi-gods depending on their culture. They were genetically enhanced by the Zetans to look physically superior to other humans so that they would be admired. The Zetans were not particularly interested in the minuscule details of daily human lives, and they left these details to the Angels. The Zetans had two commands for all their human followers.

1. Be fruitful and multiply as much as you can.
2. Wage constant wars.

These commands were designed to supply the best possible recruits for the Zetan army. Humans needed to procreate quickly to provide enough recruits, and they needed to fight among themselves so that the Zetan could pick the best recruits for their armed forces. Only a small percentage of human warriors were good enough to be enlisted into the Zetan army.

The recruitment process for the Zetan army took place on certain dates that were different in different cultures. The recruitment day was the most significant holiday for a culture. During the recruitment day, the best warriors gathered on top of a building that was visible for the rest of their tribe. On the top of the building was the Zetan or Zetans that were assigned to be gods of that culture. The angels then implanted the human chip in each of their chosen warrior and started to chant. At the height of the ceremony, the ascension process started where everyone started levitating. After that, the Zetans started their machine for dimensional travel and they all disappeared in a flash. The humans landed in a zone of the Divine Dimension where the Zetans had brought weapons and equipment. The human warriors trained in the Divine Dimension until they were ready to go to war. They were teleported the battlefield so they could fight *"the holy war against evil"* for their Zetan masters against the Xenos. Most of these humans died in battle, but a few of them retired on a distant, un-inhabited planet that was terraformed to be the ultimate human world.

Chapter 26: The End of the Multi-Millennial War.

The introduction of enlisted humans changed the tide of the conflict. The Zetan weaponry and technology were superior to that of the Xenos, and with the influx of human recruits, the Xenos could no longer capitalise on their superior numbers. The conflict was prolonged because the Xenos was adamantly against the concept of diplomacy and surrendering. The Xeno society held the idea that they were superior species, and they fought to the last individual in every battle instead of surrendering to the stronger Zetan forces.

What made it hard for the Xenos to even considering surrender was that most enemies they saw in battle were humans, a race they considered to be inferior to themselves. While this opinion was factually correct, the humans fighting for the Zetans had superior weaponry and could slowly grind down the Xenos on every planet.

3000 years after the Zetans had introduced human soldiers, their forces reached the Xeno homeworld of Xenora. With the Xenos on the brink of extinction the Xeno leadership finally decided to negotiate with the Zetans. The negotiations dragged on forever, and the delays was a deliberate plan by the Xenos. They Xenos wanted to distract the Zetans from their plan: to send a space shuttle to the star Alpha Omega, the most massive star in the galaxy located close to the centre of the Zetan galactic civilisation. The Xenos blew up Alpha Omega using a secret newly developed technology. This created a massive supernova explosion. The shockwave from this explosion annihilated the Zetan homeworld of Zetani, which signalled the end of the Zetans as a dominant race and galactic civilisation. Enraged by having their homeworld destroyed, the Zetans showed no mercy towards the Xenos and nuked the Xenora to ashes. Combined with their unwillingness to surrender this led to the supposed extinction of the Xeno species and civilization.

For the Zetans the decline came a bit slower, but it was still inevitable. The Zetans had lost their primordial Zeto Crystals, which was divine crystals containing the soul of the True Maker. The Zeto crystals had aided the Zetan abilities and made the pursue the same goal. The power of the Zeto Crystals had united the Zetans and stopped them from fighting each other.

With the Zeto Crystals gone, the Zetan civilisation was split up with every planet on its own. The Zetans on the different planets were very different genetically from each other, and without the Zeto crystals uniting them they started self-determine as separate species, and they started fighting each other. Thus, the centre of the galaxy was still inhabited, but now it was now separate species focusing on their own planets. The remaining humans from the Zetan army resettled on the planet Terra Nova, ended up fighting each other. Eventually faded to obscurity due to the limited amount of females among them.

Chapter 27: The Zetans Fight on Earth.

The Zetan gods became divided when they heard about the destruction of Zetani. They had massive egos and after millennia of praise from their human underlings, but previously the Zeto crystals had ensured that they strived for a common goal. Now that the war had ended, there was no longer any reason for them to stay close to Earth, but there was nowhere else for them to go. Their homeworld was destroyed along with most portals to the Divine Dimension. There were still a few active portals on Earth, but unfortunately, they were challenging to power up without the advanced energy sources that the Zetans had used on Zetani.

Having lost their original purpose, the remaining Zetans in the Divine Dimension got immersed in their roles as human deities. As gods, they started arguing how humans should live their lives, a question that hadn't concerned them before.

One Zetan who was very particular about governing his human followers was Yahweh, who created incredibly detailed rules for how humans should live their lives. The rules were purposefully made to contradict each other so that Yahweh could study the carnage when his followers fought bloody wars about how to interpret the rules. Watching this mayhem kept his life interesting.

As the Zeto crystals no longer unified the Zetans, they started having disagreements and fights among themselves. They chose to settle these arguments on Earth by affecting various human behaviours and betting on the outcome. The primary measure of success for the Zetans stuck in the Divine Dimension was their popularity and dominance on Earth among humanity. By making humans fight wars in their names, separate groups of Zetans could show dominance over other groups without risking the future of their species. This order worked well for the Zetans for thousands of years, until a certain event took place.

Chapter 28: Yahweh Copulates with Humans and Is Knocked Unconscious.

Before the Zetans lost their homeworld, Zetani, their sexual drive was limited and served mostly the utilitarian need to reproduce in enough numbers to keep the species alive. The influence of the Zeto crystals kept them that way as uncontrolled sexuality led to conflicts, diseases and non-optimised offspring. When they lost the Zeto Crystals, the Zetans lost their collective altruism and regressed to their biology. Hence their sexuality became a lot more prominent and with it came associated attributes such as jealousy, egotistical behaviour, and aggression.

Yahweh got obsessed with his sexuality and spent a lot of time condemning sexual behaviour among humans that he secretly craved. Yahweh was bothered by the morality of his homosexual relationship with his assistant Lucifer. The relationship caused Yahweh a lot of grief. He felt guilty for not procreating with the few Zetan women that remained, but unfortunately, they were all taken. In the end it didn't matter, as conception couldn't take place in the Divine Dimension.

Homosexuality was a new concept for the Zetans. They had been governed through the Zeto crystals for as long as records existed and in that collective mindset, sexuality was only for utilitarian purposes, to keep the species alive.

For Yahweh, his sexuality was a big issue. He felt that would eventually die, and he wanted his genetics to survive and remain forever. With no willing females of his species, Yahweh decided to make a radical move. He altered his DNA to be able to procreate with humans and used the portal to go to Earth. Doing this without consent from the other Zetans was forbidden as it took a long time to power up the portals using energy sources available on Earth.

Disobeying the other Zetans did not bother Yahweh. As he saw it, the other Zetans might kill him as retribution, but his genes would live on while theirs would eventually disappear. Once Yahweh reached Earth, he impressed many young and fertile human women with his divine powers. He promised them that that they would give birth to the great Messiah of their people. After a couple of days of non-stop sex on Earth Yahweh decided to go back to the Divine Dimension, as he was disgusted by the humans and had pushed himself hard trying to secure his legacy.

When Yahweh came back, Lucifer was furious with Yahweh's betrayal and he knocked him on conscious.

Chapter 29: The Destruction of the Zetan Portals to Earth.

When Yahweh woke up many years later, he was surrounded by a group of Zetans. Yahweh understood that they were not there because of concerns about his health.

Zeus spoke first:

- Yahweh what have you done? Lucifer told us everything; you went to Earth to have coitus with human females.

- Do you realise how dangerous that is; who knows what diseases you brought back?

Yahweh, who was temperamental, had no intention of apologising to the other Zetans, and instead he lashed out against Zeus.

Yahweh:

- Who are you to judge me? I am just doing what I must keep our genes alive.

- All the other portals are closed, and there are no means for us to travel from Earth to our former home planets.

- None of you have managed to get any offspring. It is impossible in this wretched place.

- I did what I had to do!

Lucifer:

- Your effort only led to one child. A son who was executed before he could father any children of his own. This son became worshipped like a deity after his death, so now the humans have stopped praying to us Zetans.

Yahweh:

- One? That's impossible; there should be many. I took a fertility serum before I went down there copulating with the humans.

Lucifer:

- Well, your plan failed.

Yahweh:

- I NEVER FAIL!

Yahweh was furious and grabbed his lightbringer wand which was an advanced Zetan firearm disguised as an ancient human walking stick. It was so well concealed, so the other Zetans had never realised that it was a weapon. Petrified, they watched Yahweh holding this dangerous weapon, while the rest of them were unarmed. Yahweh shouted in anger:

- Lucifer, we need to talk.
- The rest of you; LEAVE!

The other Zetans quickly left the Divine Palace.

Yahweh turned to Lucifer, who was shaking with fear. Yahweh realised that he needed to act quickly as the others was heading towards the armoury a couple of kilometres away to get their weapons. The Zetans had a rule to not store any weapons at their palaces, and this rule was a blessing for Yahweh who had enough time to execute his plan

Yahweh:

- Move it, Lucifer. We are going to the Divine Portal.

Lucifer:

- Please Yahweh, our portal to Earth is not charged yet, we will never make it to the other side.

Yahweh:

- Shut up and do what I tell you or you'll face an early grave.

Without a word, Lucifer started walking with Yahweh. They walked to the garden of the Zetan Palace. It was a marvellous place that kept beautiful plants from different planets in the Milky Way Galaxy. They walked through the garden and reached the Divine Portal to Earth. The entrance served two purposes. When it was not activated, it was just a regular gate to the vast emptiness of the Divine Dimension. When it was activated, it would teleport the person or object to Earth. They stopped in front of the gate.
Yahweh:

- Activate the portal.

Lucifer:

- Please, Yahweh. The portal is not activated on Earth, and it won't be ready for years. If we step through, we'll get disintegrated in the nothingness and die.

Yahweh:

- I know how the portal works. Just follow my instructions!
- And... Don't speak unless spoken to first!

Lucifer activated the portal, and they stood silent. The Zetan Palace was built on top of a hill and they could overlook the empty wasteland below. Originally, nothing existed in the Divine Dimension, so all the building materials including the hill the palace was built on was teleported there through the millennia by other Zetans. As nothing deteriorated in the Divine Dimension, the palace was as beautiful as when the Zetans built it eons ago.

In the distance, Yahweh could see the other Zetans returning from the armoury. It would take some time before they reached him and Yahweh studied the landscape. He looked the vast training grounds where their human forces had trained before battling the Xenos. He got nostalgic when he saw the big granaries where they had kept the offerings and sacrifices that the humans gave them. Yahweh loved to eat, and he hadn't eaten much lately.

After the destruction of the Zetan home planet, it was difficult to power the portals to Earth for non-essential visits. The portals on Earth could only slowly generate power through absorbing friction energy from Earth's orbit around the sun, but this power was not enough for regular visits. Eventually the other Zetans arrived.

Zeus:

- Yahweh! Why is the portal activated?

Yahweh:

- I am Yahweh; I don't answer to you. This palace is mine and only mine. Go to another palace and spend your time there!

Zeus:

- I don't think so.

- This palace is the only palace that has a working portal to Earth. If you surrender, we'll let you live. We'll lock you up in the Rangda's eternal prison.

Yahweh:

- I will NEVER surrender to you. Go away or I'll kill Lucifer where he stands.

Zeus:

- No one cares about your sodomite friend!
- Zetans, storm the palace and bring Yahweh's head to me!

Yahweh reacted instinctively and shot Lucifer with the force push ability on his staff. This action threw Lucifer straight into the activated Divine Portal where his body disintegrated. Additionally, the energy spike from the force push destroyed the portal, which imploded and created a tiny impassable black hole, stopping the other Zetans from entering the palace, and stopping Yahweh from leaving the palace.

Realising that they couldn't get into the palace, Zeus and the other Zetans decided to leave the Terran Palace for another palace in the Divine Dimension. Yahweh was stuck in his solitude unable to leave his self-made prison or to communicate with anyone. Eventually, he wrote his suicide letter and committed suicide. Thousands of years later, Abraham Goldstein found Yahweh's corpse.

Chapter 30: The Construction of Eden Is Completed.

Abraham Goldstein woke up after a long slumber when Lucifer contacted him. Abraham contemplated leaving the Divine Dimension so he could see Lucifer face to face, but he decided against it. His body was old and frail, and every time he woke up in the real world he could potentially die. Speaking telepathically via the divine microchips was safer although it felt less real. Abraham answered Lucifer's call:

- Yes, Lightbringer, what news do you bring me?

Lucifer:

- We have finished our construction work on Eden. It's possible to live on the surface now.

Abraham:

- Eden finalised? How did this happen so quickly?

Lucifer:

- You have been asleep for six months, Master.

Abraham:

- Why didn't you wake me up or contact me during this period?

Lucifer:

- You told me that you needed to sleep Master and that I should only disturb you if I had important news. Eden is finally inhabitable, that is outstanding news.

Abraham felt confused by Lucifer's action. He didn't know if Lucifer had used his directions to his advantage. When Abraham was asleep, Lucifer oversaw The Eden Project, and he shouldn't let this power get to his head. Abraham decided to give Lucifer more exact timelines in the future.
Abraham:

- Very well. So, nothing important happened while I was asleep?

Lucifer cleared his throat and spoke:

- On Eden everything has gone according to plan...

Abraham:

- Spit it out Lucifer, what is not going to plan?

Lucifer:

- House Goldstein have lost control of Australia to House Cheng, they conquered Sydney from us.

- Isaac Goldstein requested to stop deliveries to Eden, so that they could afford to fight back. I let him know that the Eden project was the main priority, and he should find a cheaper way to keep Australia. Apparently, Isaac failed us.

Abraham:

- He didn't fail US, Lucifer; He failed ME. You are not a Goldstein you are my bodyguard. Don't consider yourself a Goldstein; your loyalty should be to me only!

Lucifer:

- I apologise, Master; I will be more thoughtful in the future.

Abraham:

- The loss of Australia doesn't matter. We have left Earth behind us, and Eden is our future. I knew of my relatives' incompetence, and yet the fools have persisted to rebel and question my authority.

- Neither you nor any of the Angels will do the same!

Abraham's last sentence made Lucifer feel worried. He could often feel Abraham messing with his brain and reading his thoughts. Lucifer felt offended by Abraham's lack of trust. He and the other Angels had followed Abraham blindly for decades. Abraham should be courteous enough to ask questions instead of spying on his closest men.

Lucifer's thoughts were interrupted by Abraham who had read his thoughts:

- Don't be angry Lucifer; I am only looking after you and the others. Without the ability to lie to me, your souls are pure, and you can serve a higher purpose.

Lucifer:

- Thank you for showing me the light when doubt clouds my mind.

Abraham:

- Of course, you are the Light-bringer. I need you to show the way to the others.

Lucifer:

- Yes, Master!
- Would you like to wake up and visit Eden with your physical body?

Abraham:

\- No, my body is dying. I will see Eden's beauty through your eyes, my son.

Lucifer:

\- Agreed, Master. I will travel to the surface at once.

Chapter 31: Lucifer Watches Eden from the Top of Mount Sinai.

Later that day, Lucifer landed on Mount Sinai, which was a 900-meter high mountain found in the centre of Eden. Mount Sinai was where the ancient people had received their divine laws, and Abraham's followers would receive their religious laws here as well.

A fitting feature for Mount Sinai was that it was impossible to climb without "Divine Providence" This was because the atmosphere of Eden only stretched 1000 meters up. This meant that the atmospheric pressure dropped by 10 % for every 100 meters elevation from the 100 kPA at ground level to 0 kPA at 1000 meters altitude. At the top of the mountain there was only 10% air pressure, so reaching the summit of Mount Sinai without breathing aids was impossible.

Lucifer looked towards the horizon. In every direction, he could see the blackness of space where Eden ended. At surface level, the atmosphere seemed blue like on Earth but on this altitude the sky was dark like in space. Straight above him, he could see the Divine Control Centre in a fixed position 5 kilometres above Eden. In the sky, he could see the seven suns that always kept Eden in comfortable daylight. The suns were the real sun, accompanied by six large orbital space mirrors that reflected light and heat down to Eden. These mirrors could also double up as large orbital lasers that could fire powerful laser beam incinerating anything in seconds. The reason to have several large space mirrors instead of one huge was a failsafe to avoid problems if one of the mirrors got hit by debris from a passing asteroid.

When he looked down on the surface, Lucifer saw a mostly featureless and uniform terrain. Biodiversity was almost non-existent as the focus of the Eden project was to create a liveable world where Abraham could be a god, not to build a realistic replica of Earth. Lack of biodiversity was an issue that existed on all colonised worlds, as it was lot easier to make a planet liveable for humans than to create proper ecosystems.

Lucifer studied the grid-like pattern of canals and dams that would provide the inhabitants of Eden with water. While they lacked the beauty of the rivers and lakes on Earth, they were predictable and functional. There was a certain amount of water on the surface of Eden and evaporated water could not escape the atmosphere so it would always come down as rain.

Around the canals, there was farmland with farm animals and ripe produce. The farm animals had been created from fertilised eggs using synthetic wombs, and the plants was planted and kept by gardening robots. They needed to pack all this advanced technology away and store it on the dark side of Eden out of sight from Eden's future inhabitants. After all, signs of advanced technology could break the illusion of a Bronze Age civilisation honouring their supreme god.

Lucifer returned to the Divine Control Centre. He needed a good sleep, as there were busy days ahead of him. In ten days, Eden was due to be colonised by the Martian captives, and there was a lot of work to be done!

Chapter 32: Genesis.

Abraham Goldstein made the final changes to the first chapter of **The Abrahameon** his great religious work that would be the foundation for his religion. Abraham had decided to make Yahweh the great creator in his religion with himself described as Yahweh's successor. Doing this was the least he could do to honour Yahweh, as he admired everything that Yahweh had done. Abraham decided to make Yahweh the only God that was all-powerful. Abraham, as Yahweh's successor would only claim to be powerful. This distinction would not make any difference in the day-to-day life of his followers, as Abraham was still the deity to worship.

Abrahameon first chapter.

In the beginning, the great Divine Yahweh created the heavens and the Earth. After this, he created land and water; He saw that this was good. After a while, his creation started to bore him, so Yahweh created animals and plants to have something to marvel. He marvelled at the beautiful nature for millions of years.

After observing his creation through the Eons, he created humankind in his image. At first, humans were no different from the other mere beasts but eventually; Yahweh induced them with his great spirit to give them consciousness and a soul. He also introduced them to his divine law at Mount Sinai on Earth. This law was to guide them in their lives and keep them aligned to his divine plan. From the start, the foolish humans opposed him trying to live their lives in a way that was opposed to the direction given by the great Yahweh.

Yahweh kept trying to get humanity back to following his divine plan, because he loved them, and because all humans carried a bit of his soul. Having given away a part of his soul to give humanity consciousness, Yahweh suffered every time someone strayed from the path and broke against the wisdom of his divine law. Eventually, he grew older and lost his enthusiasm because of the vile abominations that humanity took part in, disrespecting his holy will.

Yahweh spoke to his Archangel and closest confidant Abraham: "Why can't I the all-powerful master of the universe get these humans to obey my will when I created them in my image?" Abraham answered: "Because you gave them a piece of your soul to give them consciousness. This part of your spirit also gave them the free will to do as they please, and stray from your path."

Having contemplated Abraham's wise words, Yahweh agreed with Abraham. He had been too kind to these people; they owed him everything, and yet they kept causing him suffering. Yahweh had lived for millions of years in peace, harmony, and bliss before creating humanity. Since he created humankind 7000 years earlier his life was nothing but pain and suffering. He summoned Archangel Abraham and his other Angels.

"I have decided to end myself and humanity." Yahweh said. After a short break, he continued, "I have suffered more these last 7000 years than I did for billions of years before humanity. These beasts have shattered my soul and I will end them, to finally find eternal peace."

The benevolent Archangel Abraham spoke up. "Grandmaster Yahweh, there are still righteous humans left on Earth that follow your divine will. We must not let them suffer" The Great Divine Yahweh answered "Abraham, the goodness of your heart is blinding you from the truth. The good deeds from the few good God-fearing humans is not even close to balance out the vile acts by the others. It is not your soul that is tormented by their actions. You don't feel it like I do" To this, Abraham replied, "You are correct, Grandmaster Yahweh. I am, however, willing to give a piece of my soul to save the worthy people of Earth when you are ready to find eternal peace in death.

Yahweh considered what Abraham had said. He suffered for the last 7000 years, and all he wanted was to end it all so that he could find peace. But destroying the good humans would be an evil deed that could ruin his peace in the afterlife. Yahweh spoke "Benevolent Archangel Abraham; I have decided to give you a year to find the good humans and bind them to your soul. I will put them asleep in a protected vessel. After that, I will kill myself and destroy Earth and everyone on it. You can take my place as the Lord of the Divine Dimension.

Everything happened as Yahweh had said. A year later Earth was destroyed in a massive flash of light. As a last gesture of his greatness, Yahweh had ended all suffering and granted the sinners a peaceful death in the afterlife. Thus, was the end of Yahweh his greatest feat of limitless love and compassion.

Abraham felt guilty as he had only found 3000 individuals on Earth worthy of salvation. Ideally, he would have wanted to give them all a second chance, but he had to follow the guidelines of his wise and all-seeing Master Yahweh. Together with his 30 angels, Master Abraham decided to create Eden as humanity's new home. Abraham promoted Lucifer to be his Archangel and his envoy to Eden while Abraham was overseeing everyone from the Divine Dimension.

The Divine Abraham decided to divide humanity into seven different tribes all living in their territory at the same distance from Mount Sinai. He appointed four angels to oversee each tribe while Archangel Lucifer oversaw all of Eden. To connect with the Divine Abraham, each newborn must have a divine shard infused with Abraham's eternal soul inserted at baptism. The infusion of this shard is the first commandment of Abraham Thy God.

Chapter 33: How Abraham Created the Angels.

Abraham Goldstein studied Lucifer through the eyes of Metatron, as Lucifer was sleeping in a sleep pod. By stimulating the neural signals of the brain during sleep, one could reduce the need to sleep from eight hours to two hours per day without any adverse side effects. Abraham had always used sleep pods, as his restless nature didn't allow him to waste a third of his days sleeping. Most individuals did not like them and preferred to sleep naturally as they needed to sleep and dream.

Lucifer and the other angels had always slept in the sleep pods as they were Abraham's aides and bodyguards, and he didn't like them wasting eight hours on sleeping every day. Abraham studied the features of Lucifer who even in his sleep glowed with charisma and leadership. All the angels had outstanding features, intelligence, and abilities but Lucifer was a man without peers. He was an exceptional individual and his uniqueness also made him potentially dangerous, and Abraham hoped that they would never turn against each other.

The first of the angels had come to be 200 years earlier when Abraham was the new CEO of Goldstein industries back on Earth. Back then it had been a humble and unassuming family business. They had been locally powerful but not omnipresent and not one the ruling houses of the Terran Council. Abraham had dreamt of becoming the wealthiest and most powerful man on the planet but to advance to that stage he needed an edge that took him ahead of his competitors.

The Angel program gave him that edge. Abraham had secretly created individuals with excellent genes and had them conceived in a synthetic womb. These individuals were kept together and isolated from the world. They were indoctrinated to be loyal to Abraham. They were also trained in all the useful skills associated with their line of work.

The Angel program was a highly secret program, and it was secret for several reasons. The most important reasons were the usage of synthetic wombs to create the individuals in the program. Artificial wombs were highly illegal for human reproduction as they created individuals that were thought to lack a soul and individuality. The reason why this happened was debated: Religious people claimed that synthetic wombs was against the divine plan while scientists argued that the issue was the inability to completely recreate the conditions a human uterus. Synthetic wombs were hardly in use on Earth as it was cheaper to create drones to do all the dangerous and monotonous work than to have soulless clones do it.

A legal reason to use synthetic wombs was for raising livestock, as it was less cruel to kill a cow without a soul than killing a cow that potentially had a soul. Artificial wombs were also used to grow body parts using stem cells, where most body parts could be regrown within a matter of weeks.

For Abraham, the lack of ego and individuality in his Angels were desirable. What he got was a group of incredibly talented people who put HIS interests before their own and was ready to give everything including their own lives, to make his will happen. The Angel Program had helped Abraham rise from a locally feared businessperson to the wealthiest and most powerful man on the planet. However, when things had deteriorated with his family, he had still been forced to leave Earth as the angels wasn't enough to protect him when everyone was against him.

Abraham saw Lucifer waking up, and he decided to let Metatron speak for him on this occasion:

Metatron:

- Wake up, Lucifer. Today is the day to populate Eden and start the eternal reign of Grandmaster Abraham.

Lucifer:

- I am ready as always, Metatron. Let's go!

Chapter 34: The First Day on Eden.

It was 8 AM on the 1st of January 2810, and the people of Eden were to be set awake after being kept asleep for 20 years. Abraham chose to align the calendars with the calendars of Earth and only change the year. The total number of individuals settled on Eden was around 3000, and they had all had their memories wiped, so all they had left was the ability to do basic movements, numeracy and language skills. They were all sleeping in their respective villages, which were replicas of Bronze Age villages from the Holy Land. All the 30 angels of Eden except for Lucifer were stationed in the hamlets under their supervision waiting for Abraham to give the signal to start.

Abraham spoke to all the Edenites through the microchips in their brains:

- Wake up people of Eden!

- You have slept for 20 years.

- You are the chosen ones, the only humans left in existence, after the apocalypse.

- The all-powerful Yahweh has destroyed himself and planet Earth. Before he did, he allowed me; Grandmaster Abraham to take his place on the Divine Throne and lead you to Eden your new home.

- Follow the Angels to Mount Sinai where you will congregate and see your new physical leader, Archangel Lucifer.

Abraham viewed the confused masses get up from their beds and aimlessly walking out. He had expected this. Memory-wiped individuals usually acted confused for a long time after being subjected to the treatment and this was to his advantage. People that were confused were less likely to question him and were easier to influence. Abraham suspected that first generation on Eden would not be easy to control. Even after a memory wipe, individuals tended to get flashbacks from their earlier lives, and these flashbacks would cause some of them to question the world they lived. They would not dare to voice their concerns, however, and after a couple of generations, he would have a group of people that believed in every word he said, through indoctrination and the lack of external stimuli.

Abraham watched the Edenites meet up in their respective villages and slowly make their way to Mount Sinai in the middle of Eden were Lucifer was preparing his speech.

Lucifer was wearing his ceremonial angel outfit while the other angels wore utility outfits. The Angels had three different uniforms depending on the purpose of their visit. They had:

- One ceremonial uniform, which was made to look extravagant, coated in gold and full of diamonds and gemstones attached in intricate patterns. This suit was highly decorative but did not serve any practical purpose except to impress.

- One utility uniform used for peacekeeping, helping villagers or fixing parts of Eden's advanced infrastructure. This suit was light blue and gave moderate protection against the elements and attacks while being mobile, lightly armed, and versatile

- One terror uniform, when Abraham wanted to punish his subjects. This suit was dark and covered the entire body including the face. It had spikes and other ornaments to make it look terrifying. It was heavily armed and designed for destruction and mayhem.

All the uniforms also had angel wings that moved to give the illusion of the angels using their wings to fly. In reality, flight thrusters under the wings gave the momentum, but the biblical angels were portrayed with wings, and Abraham liked this design feature.

The Edenites reached Mount Sinai, and the lights from the seven suns shone on Lucifer, which made him, and his gemstones shine like a beacon with the rest of Eden dimmed. He spoke to the masses, his voice amplified by speakers hidden in the mountain.

Lucifer:

- Welcome to Eden, humans. You are the last remnants of humanity.

- Humanity's terrible sins forced the great Yahweh to destroy Earth. You are alive because of the benevolence of Grandmaster Abraham, your new God.

- I am Lucifer, Abraham's Archangel and emissary on Eden. Grandmaster Abraham speaks directly through me!

- You are expected to follow the commands of Grandmaster Abraham and his angels. Comply and you will be rewarded with an honest good life. Resist and you will suffer.

- Follow the angels to your villages. They will look after you during the transition period.

- Now bow to Abraham, your new God!

As the masses bowed to Lucifer, he experienced mixed feelings; while the rush of power was intoxicating; he would have preferred a role in the background. During all his years on Earth, Lucifer had never attracted any attention. He was just a loyal servant to Abraham. It would take some time getting used to his new role, and Lucifer did not know, if he would like it or not. In the end, it did not matter, Lucifer was loyal to his master, and his master gave him this role.

Chapter 35: Jon, A typical settler on Eden.

Abraham Goldstein observed Jon of the Gad tribe who was sleeping. He could tell that Jon was unwell and confused. Jon woke up cold-sweating next to his wife, Nadia. He had experienced another strange dream that did not make any sense.

In the dream, Jon carried a rod that could fire projectiles and kill people from afar and a gadget that enabled him to speak and look at people that wasn't there. He remembered sitting in a flying ship leaving a reddish planet watching his home blow up. But nothing of this made any sense. None of these things existed, and Jon could also remember that he and Nadia had been together for years as humble farmers on Earth working hard to support their children. But if this was true, why couldn't he feel any connection to his wife nor his kids? Jon contemplated whether he was dead and life on Eden was the afterlife. The memories he had were so shallow and filled with gaps that he couldn't know what was real, and yet they were all that he had. Not finding peace, Jon quickly drank a big tankard of red wine to calm his nerves. As the intoxication took hold of him, he relaxed and fell asleep.

Jon's reaction was typical. When Abraham and the angels had wiped the memories of the first inhabitants of Eden, they had also inserted generic memories to give them a purpose and role in the society. Unfortunately, they had neither the time nor the will to provide all the Edenites with a comprehensive set of unique memories. Erasing and inserting memories was tedious, so instead of creating every individual unique they had just erased everyone's memories and used a few generic templates to create similar memories for all the Edenites. It wouldn't matter anyway; memory erosion and creation technologies could not realistically recreate and destroy a person's memories regardless of how much effort one put in. But after 50 years everyone living on Eden would be born there and all their memories would be real and prove that Abraham was their God.

The disconnection that Jon felt to his wife and children were a natural part of how Eden was set up. Abraham had made sure that all the family units on Eden consisted of individuals with no prior connection to each other. Hence, Jon, Nadia, and their three children were not connected to each other, before they were induced by memories and sent to live together in Eden. Abraham didn't want real family units, as they would share fragmented memories from their earlier lives, and they were more likely to question their current reality. When pairing individuals with no prior connection, they would all have their different memory fragments from before. However, these pieces would not match, and they would instead adapt to reality and hide their emotions.

Jon's drinking was unacceptable to Abraham. Abraham wanted his subjects to live good lives, which included being fruitful and to multiply. If Jon drank to calm his nerves, he would drink himself into an early grave and not be fruitful. If his subjects were not prolific, Abraham would run out of people to rule. Abraham decided to intervene; he activated the human chip in Jon's brain and appeared like a mirage.

Abraham:

- Jon of the Gad tribe, why are you drinking?

Jon:

- Wait, who are you?

Abraham:

- I am Abraham, thy God.

- You are abusing the gift I gave to you! I gave humanity wine, so that you can celebrate together, not to drink away your weaknesses.

Jon:

- I am sorry, Grandmaster Abraham. I repent and beg for forgiveness.

Abraham:

- Good. I forgive you sinful behaviour. For this time.

- Now honour my will and have sex with your consort. I demand you to be fruitful and multiply to praise my name!

Jon:

- I don't mean to be disrespectful, Grandmaster Abraham, but my wife and I have grown distant since you saved us and delivered us to your promised land. We have not engaged in any marital union since we arrived here.

This answer angered Abraham. This insolent human asked for help to fuck his wife. Sexuality was biology and was below his divine work. Abraham wanted to kill the audacious idiot. But that would be a pointless death, and there would be no lessons learned for the rest of the people. The first generation of inhabitants was a complete wreck and Abraham needed people born on Eden with authentic memories to gain better followers. Abraham decided to appear as a mirage to both Jon and Nadia at the same time.
Abraham:

- Wake up, Nadia!

Nadia:

- What, who are you?

Abraham:

- I am Grandmaster Abraham, Thy God!

- Jon told me that the two of you have failed to honour me by not laying together in your marital bed!

- I find this is unacceptable. I command you to have sex tonight!

Abraham made his mirage disappear and he studied Jon and Nadia. They were fumbling a bit, but they were making their way to sex. They would get there eventually; it was only biology.

Abraham concluded that the situation with Nadia and Jon was far from unique. Although he felt it was below him, he would have to face the circumstances and get his subjects to procreate. With 700 couples on Eden, this would keep him bogged down for a while. Life was not all glorious as a god.

Chapter 36: The First Birth on Eden.

Nine months after Abraham's intervention, Jon and Nadia had a baby, which was the firstborn on Eden. Abraham considered whether he should claim credit for this birth or not among the Edenites. He decided not to.

It had taken Abraham weeks to influence every couple on Eden and ensure that their sex lives were flourishing. If people believed that his influence was necessary for them to conceive, they would regularly petition him for help. Being asked for favours was NOT how Abraham wanted to rule as a god. He wanted his subjects to worship, obey and fear him; he had no interest in being a wish-granting genie that was evoked to solve trivial matters in his subjects' lives.

Abraham was relieved that his subjects were able to procreate. Although he had not foreseen any reasons why their reproductive health would be dysfunctional; It was unknown what effects the combination of memory wiping and spending an extended period cryogenically frozen would have on the human reproduction system. There had been earlier expeditions to other star systems where people had procreated once they landed but these expeditions had brought advanced technology aiding human reproduction while his Eden project did not.

Abraham commanded Jon and Nadia to name their firstborn daughter Lillian. Abraham chose this name, to honour his late wife Lillian Goldstein. However, he left this part out of the narrative. It did not fit the story that the divine and eternal Grandmaster Abraham was mourning his dead wife.

Abraham commanded everyone on Eden to attend the baptism of Lillian. As she was the first-born on Eden, her baptism would set the ceremony for all future childbirths. The baptism was led by the Angel Gabriel, who oversaw the Gad tribe. The masses sang a song to praise Abraham for his mercy to save humanity. Gabriel splashed water on the head of the newborn to symbolise that water was the source of all life. After doing this, he inserted a human chip in the newborn so that the Angels and Abraham would able to communicate and read the mind of their new subject. Gabriel described the microchip as a part of the Grandmaster Abraham's soul that he gave all newborn babies to bless them. Finally, Gabriel made a small cut in the child's finger to drop blood on the stone of eternity, which was an advanced DNA analyser disguised as an ornamental rock.

Abraham was satisfied with the ceremony. The baptism ritual went through without any incident, and it solved two practical issues:

- It made sure everyone had a divine technology microchip in their heads.
- It gathered DNA from every individual.

Collecting DNA from individuals was important for Abraham as it allowed him to further his understanding of how the behaviour of his subjects was linked to their genetics. It also provided him with a framework for how he could utilise selective breeding to alter the features of future generations without using modern technology. The genetics of everyone on Eden was saved in the mainframe for future research.

Chapter 37: The Priests of Eden.

During the first year on Eden, the angels were always at the surface helping and leading the tribes they were supervising. Doing this had a drawback, however, eventually they would age and die. Abraham wanted his Eden project to last for an eternity. For this to happen, the angels needed to be cryogenically frozen most of the time. Abraham estimated that the lifespans of his angels when combining cryogenic sleep and DNA regeneration technology would be thousands of years. With a bit of luck, the rest of humanity would be extinct by then so that Abraham would be the god of all humankind.

Abraham decided to pick the most suitable family of each tribe to become the head priests. Abraham used his DNA database to decide who would be the best head priest for a tribe. Abraham decided that he would not allow female leaders. Female leaders were a poison that he had experienced too much on Earth. The ancients were wise by only allowing male clerics. Allowing female clerics was one of the factors destroying religion back on Earth.

As Eden was a theocracy, the head-priest was the ruler of the tribe. Appointing governors for the tribes saved Abraham time as he could communicate to the leaders to make them do his bidding, instead of talking to every human individually. It was also good to have an earthly power in place to keep some of the mystique around himself and his angels. If a ruler for some reason displeased him, he could always choose to kill them quietly by causing a brain haemorrhage or make a public display by having them executed. No man on Eden, not even the local leaders, were above God, and their life and well-being was dependent on pleasing Abraham and doing his will.

After setting up the religious leadership on Eden, Abraham ordered the angels to return to the Divine Control Centre where they could spend most of their time in suspended animation to extend their lives. Happy with his achievements, Abraham moved to his meditation spot in the Divine Dimension and meditated for ages; letting the humans of Eden govern themselves for a while.

Chapter 38: A Childhood Nightmare.

Lucifer had one of his recurring nightmares. In the dream, he was a young child and today was the day he entered adulthood. Everyone was looking at him when he took the oath that his childhood was over, and he swore to serve Master Abraham for the rest of his life. A man was brought in to him. He was chained and beaten. The man was pleading for mercy. Lucifer's mentor gave Lucifer a loaded gun and told him to kill the prisoner to prove his loyalty. Lucifer felt sick, he had never killed before and he did not know, that this was one his tasks. He searched the room for his best friend, but there were no children in the hall today; only adult Angels screaming for blood. Lucifer raised the pistol and screamed his lungs out as he shot the prisoner with many bullets. With blood on his face, Lucifer caught the gaze of the dying prisoner. Lucifer swallowed the vomit that was coming up from his throat, as he could not allow himself to show weakness.

Lucifer woke up, and he could still see the gaze of the murdered prisoner staring into his soul. His adulthood ceremony had scarred him for life, and he had never shared his feelings with anyone.

For Lucifer, his adulthood ceremony was a shocking revelation on how his life was meant to be. He was brought up in the Angel program, and this was all he knew about, but until that day he was taught mostly physical perfection and science. Lucifer's mentor told him that Master Abraham had selected Lucifer to be one of his guardians which was a fancy title for a bodyguard.

An Angel was considered adult and eligible for active duty at the age of 13 although for practical reasons they usually started active duty when they were around 20. During his years on Earth, Lucifer had killed countless individuals for Abraham, and yet it was always the first murder that came back to haunt him.

What bothered Lucifer was that he never found out why he killed the prisoner on his adulthood ceremony. There was no record explaining why they had killed him. This was often the case as the angels killed on direct orders from Abraham Goldstein, and there was no reason to keep records. After all, too much record-keeping could expose what they were doing. Lucifer never bothered to find out what his other victims had done, but the first one was a splinter in his mind that he could not heal from.

Unable to find peace, Lucifer entered a cryogenic tank and set the timer for six months. Hopefully, such a long time in the tank would get his mind off the matter. Regardless, he was not needed in the day-to-day operation of Eden now that everything was up and running and the others would wake him up if he was needed. Lucifer felt the cold of the helium mixture flowing in before it was a snap, and everything turned dark.

To be cryogenically frozen was like being killed and then resuscitated upon waking up. As no decay could happen on the cellular level in the freezing temperatures of the tank, this was a way to preserve a person indefinitely. While older technologies sometimes failed to resuscitate the user, the technologies used in the 29th century were very safe.

Chapter 39: A Plot Against Abraham.

James Goldstein was a 10th generation descendant of Abraham Goldstein and a low-level manager at House Goldstein. Since he was a Goldstein, he owned a small share of the company and had voting rights at the Annual General Meeting. As James Goldstein was a young child in 2785 when Abraham carried out his coupe, James had no divine technology chip inserted. Thus, his mind could not be read, and Abraham could not kill him remotely. He looked at a picture of his late parents. Abraham had murdered them using the divine technology chip. But James was not driven by revenge; he was motivated by ambition.

James was 29 years old in the year 2812. Abraham murdered James' parents in the year 2786 before he left Earth. Thus, James had very faint memories of them and instead his maternal aunt who was not a Goldstein had raised him. He grew up under humble circumstances far away from the excess and abundance of the Goldstein Tower. While no Terran citizen was poor, James had grown up in relative poverty compared to everyone around him, and he had dreamt about living in the excess and abundance of Goldstein Tower.

Upon reaching adulthood, James was able to access his parent's estate, which was in a trust fund during his childhood. Eager to live a life of luxury and excess, he was thoroughly disappointed once he got to live and work in Goldstein Tower. The place was in shambles with cracks in the walls and old worn out furniture. The food and beverage were not much better than he had received while growing up in poverty and the totality of his parent's estate was not worth more than 100,000 Terran Credits, or ten years of average pay.

James found out that wealth of House Goldstein was depleted due to the excessive spending on the Eden project. James hatched a plan. If he could depose Abraham from power, he could make a move for the top. This plan was counting on a swift and brutal retaliation from Abraham, which would kill off most of the senior members of House Goldstein. By moving in swiftly after their deaths, James planned to grab as much estate as he possible could, while the unprepared descendants of House Goldstein would lose out. This would push James to a position of power in the company or at least to a much higher position.

After spending the last five years finding accomplices, James was ready to make a move for power.

Chapter 40: Breaking News.

Terran Global News 5th August 2812:

A massive explosion occurred today at Goldstein Tower destroying the top five levels of the building and killing dozens on the ground from the debris. The cause of the explosion hasn't been determined, but it is speculated to be a targeted attack aimed to kill the elusive Abraham Goldstein, founder and majority shareholder of House Goldstein who has remained unseen for the last 20 years.

One of the Security Managers for House Goldstein, James Goldstein has confirmed that Abraham Goldstein died in the explosion, and he released a video of Abraham Goldstein conversing with his bodyguards before the bombing.

As the blast vaporised Abraham's body, there is no way to resurrect him. Abraham's death marks the end of 272-year-old stalwart who outlived most of his descendants.

Abraham's death is bad news for House Goldstein that has struggled and lost most of their influence and wealth during the reign of Isaac Goldstein. Analysts speculate about an upcoming and unpredictable power struggle within the company, which could lead to its demise. More updates and commentary on the subject to come!

Chapter 41: Abraham's peace is shattered.

Abraham was meditating under the ever-blooming Lotus Tree in the Divine Dimension. Initially, it had surprised him that he enjoyed the stillness and the vastness of the infinite, more than overlooking his subjects but then it had dawned on him: The old Abraham was no more. The Abraham of Earth had limited time to achieve what he wanted, so he had never allowed himself to let things go. Once Abraham had attained godhood, he got a new outlook on life. With near infinite power over his subjects and unlimited time, control was less important, and he allowed himself to meditate for months on end.

Suddenly, Abraham felt a burning headache that shattered the peace and knocked him to the ground. He screamed his lung out in pain, but no one answered his calls as he was the only one there. Eventually, the pain diminished, and he got back to his senses. The pain reminded him of the insignificant nibbling he felt every time someone on Eden died. But this time it felt a thousand times more intense. Had something happened to one of his angels? He could feel the connection to all the angels on Eden but from the ones on Earth it was only static. Abraham contacted Nuriel:

- Nuriel I feel a great disturbance in the force. Have you spoken to the Angels on Earth?

Nuriel:

- I haven't spoken to them, our orbit is too far away from Earth for our telepathic connection to work, and Earth is on the other side of the sun which blocks our encrypted messages. We received a message from them one week ago, and back then everything was going according to plan

Abraham:

- I see, can you contact them now?

Nuriel:

- No, I can't They will be blocked by the sun's electromagnetic inter-ference zone for another week.

Abraham:

- This is an emergency. Contact them via Spacenet.

Spacenet was the 29th-century interplanetary networks covering every nook and cranny of the solar system. Spacenet consisted of thousands of satellites in different orbits around the sun, and it made it possible to always contact every human settlement regardless of their relative position towards each other. It was developed through the centuries to avoid problems arising when settlements came into radio shadow caused by the sun or other celestial objects. It was rarely used for transmitting sensitive information as it had limited capabilities for secure encryption. This was because the quantum computing power and AI at the time was so advanced, so any encrypted message could be decrypted. The computing power was not an issue in the 29th century, but the speed of light was. Thus, every satellite contained a clone of the entire public part of Spacenet to improve usage speeds. Sending a message to another part of the solar system, however, could take hours, based on the distance between the two colonies.

Abraham navigated Spacenet through the eyes of Nuriel and he checked the distance to Earth. Earth was 45 light minutes away from Eden so the earliest response he could get was in 1.5 hours. Deciding to pass the time, Abraham read the news to find out what was happening on Earth. Finding out about the explosion at Goldstein Tower and his presumed death was too much for Abraham who passed out from the shock.

Chapter 42: The Resurrected Abraham Faces Problems.

Abraham was floating in the vast darkness of the afterlife. This place was timeless, and he did not mind being here at all. Abraham was dead and with the death came the separation of the ego and the soul. In the distance he could hear the calling *"Master Abraham, can you hear me?"* The calling became louder and eventually Abraham woke up in the Divine Control Centre experiencing excruciating pain. His vision and hearing were blurred, but he perceived that Lucifer and few of his angels were next to his cryogenic tank. Abraham tried to call out, but he could not make a sound. A flash of light struck his eyes, and he was back in the Divine Dimension.

Lucifer:

- Master Abraham, can you hear me?

Abraham:

- Yes, I can hear you. What happened?

Lucifer:

- You died, Master. You have been dead for a year.

Abraham:

- What! How did this happen?

Lucifer:

- Nuriel said that your relatives' betrayal, and the deaths of Malphat, Hashmallim, Seraphim, and Ishmael, was too much for you, so you died from grief.

- When I woke up, your body was beyond saving, but your brain was still preserved due to the freezing cold of the cryogenic tank.

- We had to replace your body with a robotic body, and the only part of you that remains is your brain.

Abraham:

- I see. How come that I have been dead for a year?

Lucifer:

- Because we couldn't get the proper equipment. It would be suicidal to land on Antarctica and asking House Goldstein. We did not dare to approach the other factions, as we were unaware of the current allegiances on Earth. We scouted the black market for the necessary equipment. Eventually, we acquired the hardware needed. As it turned, out we had some untouched bank accounts from our secret operations 25 years ago.

Abraham:

- I see. Thank you very much Lucifer, you are a great man.

Lucifer:

- Thank you, Grandmaster Abraham.

- Unfortunately, there is a complication. We are broke. In your absence, we haven't been able to find a way of funding the Eden project. Without funding, we will not be able to buy the necessary spare parts to support Eden.

Abraham:

- I feared as much. Leave it with me, Lucifer, I will find a solution. I didn't become the wealthiest man in the solar system for nothing!

Chapter 43: Abraham Starts Trafficking Children.

Abraham was sitting on his throne in the Divine Dimension, hoping to come up with a solution to the economic hardship of the Eden project. He was struggling to think clearly as the phantom pains in his body proved hard to disconnect. He had seen his robotic body once, through the eyes of Lucifer, and he did not want to see it again. It was a contraption and an eyesore. While he could stay awake and move around in the regular dimension, he did not want to. The normal dimension was imperfect while the Divine Dimension was perfection. Regardless he could see anything he wanted from there, through controlling his angels and sharing their vision.

Abraham managed to let go off the phantom pains from, and he was struck by frustration instead. The frustration was aimed inwards instead of outwards. Abraham usually blamed everything that did not go according to plans on someone else, but this time it was different. This time he admitted that he had made a critical mistake.

Successfully subduing all the resistance within his own faction, he had failed to account for time and plan long-term. He should have predicted that there would be future Goldstein's, who were not chipped, and had he should have taken precautions against them. Instead, his short-sightedness had put him in a very tricky spot.

Ideally, Abraham would return to Earth proving that he was still alive. Unfortunately, the loss of his physical body meant that he was dead according to Terran law and the division of his assets would have continued.

Abraham realised that he should have hidden enormous amounts of money into slush funds that he controlled. Even when he "died" these assets would not be distributed to his relatives and he could have supported the Eden Project indefinitely. Unfortunately, he had not taken this precaution.

Eventually, it dawned on Abraham what he needed to do. He needed to deal with an old enemy of House Goldstein. As the rest of House Goldstein had turned against him, his former enemy could turn out to be his future friend.

It was a poorly kept secret that the Chairman of House Rashid, Ibrahim Rashid, liked young girls; incredibly young girls. Ibrahim Rashid had been threatened with expulsion from the Terran Council if he did not keep his perverted compulsions at bay. He had agreed to this, knowing that every Terran citizen had a tracking chip implanted so he was unable to spend time with children without this being detected by the Terran Council.

What if Abraham could fund the maintenance of the Eden project by selling unregistered children to Ibrahim Rashid? House Rashid could afford it, as the expensive part was to create Eden, the maintenance was less expensive.

Abraham decided to contact Ibrahim Rashid via the hologram generator. Abraham computer-generated a hologram of himself speaking to Ibrahim, as he did not want not to share his current appearance with his former enemy.

Abraham:

- Ibrahim! Inshallah, it has been too many years since the last time we spoke.

- As you know, my treacherous family destroyed my home at Goldstein Tower and declared me dead to split my assets.

- I am alive, but I have no intention of going back to Earth.

- I need financial aid, and I request a 1 billion Terran Credits interest-free loan to complete the Eden project and regain control over my faction.

- In return, I will provide you with unregistered and very well-maintained young virgins. Please get back to me as soon as possible.

After sending the message, Abraham sat back and relaxed. The message would take 45 minutes to reach Ibrahim Rashid and then the same time to come back. Interplanetary communications were not for the impatient!

A few hours later, Abraham received a response from Ibrahim Rashid:

- Greetings Lucifer of House Goldstein. I did not become the leader of House Rashid by being gullible. Abraham Goldstein has been dead for over 20 years.

- I am considering helping you. But I do request that you are forthcoming with me. I do not know what your agenda is, but it is hurting House Goldstein, which has always been rivals of House Rashid.

- I require that you show yourself. Do this, and we will talk, try to fool me again, and our conversation is over.

At first, Abraham felt angry when he received Ibrahim's message. His ego was offended by the notion that he was dead, and that Lucifer would be shrewd enough to usurp power within House Goldstein. Lucifer had many good qualities, but ambition was not one of them.

After a while, Abraham realised that being "dead" on Earth had advantages. He was disliked on Earth, and yet no other faction had interfered with the Eden project since its inception decades ago. Being 'dead' on Earth was ideal as it left him to focus on his Eden project without interruptions. Abraham summoned Lucifer to the communications room.

Lucifer:

- You summoned me, Master?

Abraham:

- Yes, I need your help to solve our financial problems.
- I need you to call Ibrahim Rashid for me.

Lucifer:

- Ibrahim Rashid? Why would we contact that filthy paedophile? The Rashid's have always been our enemy.

Abraham:

- Lucifer! Don't question your Master!

- Ibrahim Rashid is an enemy of House Goldstein. But we are enemies of the remaining Goldstein's'. The enemy of my enemy is my friend.

- Ibrahim agreed to lend us 1 Billion Terran Credits, which I can invest, to cover the upkeep of Eden indefinitely.

Lucifer:

- I see, and what does that snake want in return?

Abraham:

- He wants to communicate with you. He believes that I am dead and that you are in charge.

- We'll play along with this, but don't get any ideas.

- Tell him your Terran name and show your face to him, he requested transparency.

After this conversation, Lucifer connected to the hologram creator to communicate with Ibrahim Rashid. The hologram generators of the 29th century was very advanced as they used Nanotechnology replicating the outer layer of a person to give the feeling that the person was in the room. To verify his identity, Lucifer also attached a sample of his DNA to the message.
Lucifer:

- Dear Mr Rashid.

- This is Terence Lowenstein, known by my operative name, Lucifer. You have requested to communicate with me.

- Please, tell me, what can I do to secure your aid for our project?

When Ibrahim Rashid received the message an hour later, he was a bit perplexed about Lucifer's identity. There was a character match for Terence

Lowenstein, but there were almost no records on the activities of Terence Lowenstein. He had left Earth over two decades ago on the same date as Abraham Goldstein. He was back to Antarctica a few years later, to disappear again. He had, however, spent the last six months on Earth and had recently left the planet.

Surprisingly, Terence Lowenstein had no personal assets on Earth or anywhere else in the solar system. If he had siphoned House Goldstein for money, he was either good at hiding his assets, or he was not the one behind internal strife and rapid decline of House Goldstein. But, if supporting Lucifer could bring House Goldstein down, it was worth it, no matter who he was, or what his end goal was. Ibrahim transmitted another message:

- Very well, Terence.

- Although I know who you are, I still don't know your agenda.

- But you are the enemy of my enemy, and as such you are my friend.

- I will issue you an interest-free loan of 1 Billion Terran Credits. To receive the money, you need to assassinate the chairman of House Goldstein, Isaac Goldstein.

- Let me know when it's done.

An hour later, the message reached Eden. Lucifer was about to answer when Abraham stopped him.
Abraham:

- No, Lucifer. We are not killing Isaac Goldstein.

Lucifer:

- But why, Master Abraham? Your body is no longer an issue. You can travel to Earth and kill Isaac with your mind. The money will be yours, and Eden's future will be secured.

Abraham:

- Do you really think Isaac Goldstein was behind the attack at Goldstein Towers?

- The angels at Goldstein Tower could read all the board members minds, and yet they were taken by surprise.

- This means that our enemy us was not chipped and had nothing to fear.

- If we kill the chipped board members, nothing will stop the rest of House Goldstein to send their fleet to annihilate us.

- So, Isaac Goldstein needs to live along with the rest of the board. He is only valuable to us as a hostage.

Lucifer:

- I am sorry, Master Abraham. You are right.

Abraham:

- This I what we will do

- You'll refuse to kill the Goldstein board, as it's unwise to kill the incompetent board members, who bringing the company down.

- You'll also deliver a 9-year-old virgin to Ibrahim's private holiday residence orbiting Earth, as a token of goodwill.

Lucifer:

- What? You want to give a child to that child molester? That's insanely immoral

As this was the second time Lucifer spoke up against him, Abraham lost his temper and he knocked Lucifer to the ground with a psionic blast.
Abraham:

- Silence you fool. I AM YOUR MASTER!

- We need money. Otherwise, Eden will be destroyed, and all our subjects will die.

- Our people need to find their way back to our roots, we are the bearer of Yahweh's legacy, and I am the Chosen One to make it happen.

- Individuals are expendable, it's only the group that matters.

- Now do my bidding.

Lucifer:

- Yes, Master.
- Your will shall be done.

Chapter 44: The agreement between Abraham Goldstein and Ibrahim Rashid.

Upon receiving the first child bride, Ibrahim Rashid was overwhelmed with joy. The girl a lot purer than the filth he had ever experienced in the orbiting brothels on the fringes of the solar system. Better yet, she was free from the Martian diseases and radiation issues. Furthermore, as she was not of Terran descent, she was unregistered and not chipped, meaning he could keep her in secret at his orbital vacation residence.

Ibrahim was a bit worried about the Terran Council finding out about the girl, but he shrugged it off. The men working at his private residence was loyal and would not betray him to the ungodly and morally bankrupt other factions. Following the rites of his ancient spiritual guide, Ibrahim Rashid named the girl Alisha and married her according to the old customs of his people. He consummated the marriage later the same day. While the poor little girl was bleeding and crying in the corner, Ibrahim Rashid patted his own fatty belly pleased with himself.

Ibrahim decided to lend Terrence Lowenstein the 1 billion Terran credits that he asked for. The terms agreed was that the loan would run interest-free over 18 years, and instead of paying interest Lucifer would supply Ibrahim with a total of 72 virgins over those 18 years. If the Kaffirs for some reason could not pay back the billion at the end of the loan Ibrahim's armed forces would annihilate them, and Ibrahim Rashid made this clear. Eventually, Ibrahim Rashid dozed off and fell asleep.

Once the money was secured, Abraham invested them and he made enough money to support Eden forever. After all, his greatest strength had always been to predict how the market would develop, and this was how he had created his immense wealth in the first place.

Chapter 45: Of Virgin Blood and Divine Sky.

Humankind despite Grandmaster Abraham's effort was still soiled by the ancestor's sins that destroyed our homeworld; Earth.

Master Abraham sayeth: Thou shall slowly cleanse your sin by giving up that, which is pure and loved by all. Bring thy daughters while they are pure untouched by men and have not yet bled. Thy Lord Abraham shall each season pick a bride to bring to his divine realm and slowly cleanse the sin of humanity by forming a union with the virgin. This shall happen until the debt is repaid and the balance is restored.

Abrahameon: Chapter 23 paragraph 7

Lucifer closed the Abrahameon, the holy book for Eden. It was a work in progress. Lucifer was sickened by this chapter, and he strongly disagreed with Abraham' decision to sign a deal with the devil, Ibrahim Rashid. Regardless, there was not much Lucifer could about it. The deal was made, and Ibrahim Rashid had threatened that he would bring his army and destroy Eden if he did not receive what he was promised.

Neither Eden nor the Divine Control Centre was fearsome battle stations. They had enough defences to deter any raiders, pirates, or Martians from daring to approach. But the defences weren't designed to withstand a full-scale attack from a hostile fleet. On the flip side, if they kept House Rashid happy, they were protected from the weakened remains of House Goldstein.

It was time again, time for another innocent girl to be sacrificed for the greater good. Three years had passed, so today's offering would be the 12th to be sent as blood payment to the demented Ibrahim Rashid. Lucifer pitied the girl that would be selected. He tried to avoid thinking about her fate, was it a death sentence or something much worse?

On the selection day, every eligible Edenite girl were summoned to a platform covered in hologram technology or "the blue light of God". They were stripped naked and had to stand that way for the "selection" to take place. This took several hours, as the distance to Earth made transferring the holograms to Ibrahim time-consuming. Once Ibrahim, hade made his decision, all the blue lights was aimed at the selected girl, who was put in a portable cryogenic tank and shipped off to Ibrahim 's private residence.

Lucifer had met Ibrahim Rashid once when delivering one of the unlucky tribute girls. Ibrahim had invited him for a tour of his home, and Lucifer had agreed. Suddenly, Lucifer had been encapsulated in a transparent force field that stopped him from moving. Horrified, Lucifer was forced to watch as the hairy and fat Ibrahim raped his latest victim. During this whole gruesome act, Ibrahim had stared him down to assert his dominance. After completion, the vile monstrosity had dragged the poor girl to another room of the building. After that, Ibrahim's guards evicted Lucifer from the residence. During the two-week trip back to Eden, Lucifer had made plans for revenge and justice. Ibrahim's home was not that well-guarded, and Lucifer and the other angels were trained killers and would be capable of killing Ibrahim and his guards.

Abraham had read Lucifer's mind and reprimanded him. Killing Ibrahim Rashid would kill their only ally and would bring a fleet of House Rashid spaceships to destroy Eden. That was a battle that could not be won. While Ibrahim was a vile man, he was too important to get rid of. The suffering by the few was necessary to bring a good life to the many. Lucifer could not understand how Abraham's action would bring a good life to the people. Abraham replied:

- Do not question, Lucifer. Just dedicate your faith to your Master. You are the jewel of my creation and if you just believe in me and never question, all the answers will come.

Lucifer went to his cryogenic tank and thought back on those words. *"Never question, and all the answers will come".* He had stayed loyal for 30 years on this bloody rock, and Lucifer was none the wiser. Resigning to his fate, he sighed before experiencing the quick chill of the cryogenic tank for a long good sleep.

Chapter 46: The Disconnect Deepens.

Abraham Goldstein was struggling to focus and be satisfied with life. Despite having all the power, he had ever dreamt of he was not satisfied. In fact, he was severely frustrated: Sexually frustrated.

For the last 120 years, Abraham never had sex. It wasn't appealing to him although it was available to him due to his wealth and the right pharmaceuticals. Abraham's physician had explained, that a common side effect of the DNA regeneration technology was the lack of sexual drive once the individual had reached the end of his natural lifespan. It had not bothered Abraham at the time. He was very sexually active during the first 130 years of his life and with the sexual drive gone he could focus his energy on expanding his wealth and power.

Since Abraham had lost his body, Abraham's sex drive had changed, and sex became important again. He realised that this was because his new body made it impossible to have physical sex, and thus it became more important to him. Abraham fulfilled his sexual urges by watching people having sex. This became an addiction to him and filled him with unfulfilled desires. From the Divine Dimension, he could connect to all the humans and watch them have sex. The worst part was of studying people's sex lives were the Sodomites.

Sodomy was very uncommon on Earth during Abraham's lifetime, and it had never bothered him that much. While sodomy was not illegal on Earth, it was uncommon due to laws and regulations surrounding births and conceptions. Every individual on Earth had a set of bionic microchips controlling many aspects of their life. One of these chips acted like a permanent birth control device that prevented unplanned pregnancy.

To get pregnant, an individual needed permission from the authorities, which recommended DNA optimisation for every child. The DNA optimisation gave the child the "best" genetic output based on the parent's DNA. One of the genetics that was usually deselected was the genetic for homosexuality.

This meant that only 5 individuals in a million, was gay in the 28th Century. On Mars, where genes were spread naturally, the prevalence of homosexuality was between 5-10 per cent of the population; like the ratio on Earth in the 21st century. Since the Edenites descended from Martians, they also had about 5-10 per cent homosexuals.

Abraham was against homosexuality while his sexual addiction made him fascinated by the concept. He remembered Yahweh's suicide letter, and he realised the dangers that he faced. Abraham decided to do two things:

- He would have a chemical castration drug injected into his brain to get rid of his sexual obsession.
- He would punish the sodomites following the scriptures and the ancient law.

Abraham wanted to justify punishing the homosexuals among the Edenites. Unfortunately, nothing in the Abrahameon stated that homosexuality was a sin or forbidden, as Abraham had been oblivious to the issue. Eventually, Abraham found a way to justify punishment of homosexuals. He contacted Lucifer:

- Lucifer, I am angry with you.

Lucifer:

- Grandmaster Abraham. I don't understand. How have I angered you?

Abraham:

- You have failed to punish the Sodomites for their ungodly behaviour!

Lucifer:

- The Sodomites? What group is that and what have they done?

Abraham:

- The homosexuals, men who lay with men and women with women!

Lucifer:

- Oh...

Lucifer and the other angels were asexual and had little interest in sex. Abraham had designed their DNA this way, to keep them focused on doing the missions he gave them. To be on the safe side, the angels also had microchips that repressed their sexuality. Lucifer had no idea why the homosexuals was an issue or why he was supposed to punish them and he answered Abraham:

- Abraham, I wasn't instructed to keep track of the Edenites' sexual habits and I cannot recall anything in Abrahameon that forbids homosexuality.

Abraham:

- One of my most important commandments in the Abrahameon is "Be fruitful and multiply." Choosing a life of sodomy is a clear intention to break that rule. Hence the culprits need to be punished!

- Gather the angels, dress for punishment and terror; I will make everyone gather at Mount Sinai.

- I will instruct you further, once you are in position. Now go!

Hearing this, Lucifer rushed to get him and the other angels ready for immediate deployment to Eden.

Chapter 47: Death to the Sodomites.

Yehuda was a farmer and a father of eight children. He lived a good life following the decrees of the Abrahameon and to reward this, Lucifer had promoted him to become the high priest for his tribe. While Lucifer and the other angels had been very present during the first years on Eden, their presence became less and less noticeable as the years passed by. 20 years after Yehuda and his family woke up on Eden, the angels were only spotted sporadically. They usually came to solve problems or to collect offerings.

Yehuda had lost one of his daughters in the selection. Her name was Helena, and she had been one of the cutest girls on Eden. Yehuda felt bittersweet about his loss. While it was a great honour that Abraham chose Helena to accompany him in heaven, it was sad to not see her grow up and have a family.

Yehuda often wondered what happened to the chosen girls after the selection. He had asked Lucifer, who had told him that he should be happy for Helena. Grandmaster Abraham had selected his daughter to receive direct entry to heaven while most people had to follow the Abrahameon strictly and live a good life to reach heaven when they died. As Helena was picked while she was still pure, she was saved from the horrors and torment of hell that awaited sinners when they died.

Although this had relieved Yehuda of his worst woes, it also confused him. Lucifer had mentioned that Helena was in paradise with Grandmaster Abraham. But on another occasions, Lucifer had told Yehuda that the enchanted cylinder that selected girls entered before leaving Eden was to prevent them from suffocating.

But if the only way for a human to reach paradise were to die, why would Lucifer bring an enchanted cylinder to stop the selected girls from suffocating? Yehuda concluded that some things were not understandable for ordinary men, and that Grandmaster Abraham had a plan that benefitted everyone on Eden.

While Yehuda missed Helena but was happy for her eternal salvation; Yehuda was concerned about his son Simon. Yehuda had tried to arrange a marriage for Simon so he could be fruitful and multiply. Simon had refused, as he insisted that his true love was a man named Christopher. Simon's homosexuality broke Yehuda's heart, and he hoped that Simon would not face eternal damnation in hell for his desires.

Choosing, a life of sodomy was against the commandment that humans should be fruitful and multiply. Simon had brushed off his father's concern and replied that Grandmaster Abraham wanted everyone to love and be loved, and since he was created this way, there was no way his love could be sinful. Besides, there was no explicit ban on homosexuality in the Abrahameon.

Failing to convince Simon about his mistake, Yehuda still loved him and tried to introduce him to different women, hoping that one of them would trigger his natural desire to procreate. Yehuda had even pleaded with Lucifer to cure Simon's affliction. Lucifer had not shown the issue much interest and had stated that Yehuda's other six children seemed well adapted and with Grandmaster Abraham's blessings Yehuda's bloodline was bound to expand and prosper in the future. Grandmaster Abraham did not expressively forbid sodomy, and Lucifer could not care less how the humans of Eden were directing their sexual energies.

Suddenly, Grandmaster Abraham appeared like a mirage in the room. He commanded Yehuda to gather all the villagers at once and head for Mount Sinai. Once they reached Mount Sinai, they realised that it would not be a friendly announcement. There were fire and smoke around the mountain, and the angels were dressed in terrifying black armour with spikes and blood. Fear and confusion spread among the villagers that had to stand in anticipation until everyone had arrived.

Once everyone was gathered, Abraham appeared as a gigantic illusion standing above the angels. He was wearing his usual robe and cane but to signify the importance of today's assembly he was also wearing his divine crown. Abraham's eyes were burning with anger and his voice shouted out.

- People of Eden. Too many of you engage in ungodly behaviours.

- I have commanded you to be fruitful and multiply, and yet many of you pursue practices that contradict this command!

- Yes, I talk about men who sleep with men, women with women, bestiality and other sick practices that I have witnessed being an all-seeing god

- This must end today. The following people step forward.

Abraham started shouting out names. He was aware of a total of 300 homosexuals out of the current population that had risen to 6000. While it would be convenient to wipe them all out at once, Abraham wanted to instil fear. Besides by outing all the homosexuals and punish some of them publicly, he was sure to get some entertainment later when the religious mobs of Eden made short work of any undesirables.

Abraham instructed the angels to divide the sodomites into two groups. One group consisted of 60 individuals and the other consisted of 240 persons. The 60 were the condemned ones, and Abraham read out the allegations for everyone to hear. Yehuda's son, Simon, was one of them. "*Not only had Simon, son of Yehuda chosen to perform unnatural acts with men, but he had done so against his father's wishes and disregarded all attempts to change his mind and lay with a woman which was the natural thing to do. For such a wicked sinner, there was only one way to go, to be cleansed by fire.* "

The 60 condemned sodomites were placed on an elevated platform surrounded by an invisible forcefield that stopped them from leaving. They were then slowly roasted in front of the crowds by an orbiting laser. The smell of burnt flesh was covering the valley. But Abraham was not going to let them have a swift death. So, the fires were extinguished, and stimulants and oxygen pumped into the area to ensure that everyone was awake and suffering. This process went on for three hours, and eventually Abraham had seen enough. He set the lasers to full effect and killed the condemned.

Abraham:

- Remember this day people of Eden! Every year on this day 60 sodomites will burn on this mountain. You need to deliver them to me. If you do not do so, it's because you are protecting these abominations. If you do more of you will suffer!

Chapter 48: Lucifer's Dilemma.

Lucifer felt uncomfortable over the things that had happened. Although he understood why Abraham wanted to eradicate the homosexuals the way it had played out was indefensible. The orbital lasers were powerful and could incinerate a man in seconds; it would have been a clean and almost painless death. Instead, Abraham roasted the condemned ones for hours on end for no other reasons than sadistic ones.

The solution was senseless. If Abraham wanted to eradicate the problem, he could have killed all the homosexuals at once. Instead, he murdered one-fifth of them and gave the others a death sentence by proclaiming that 60 homosexuals should be killed every year. The knowledge about their damnation was worse than a swift death, and Lucifer pitied the condemned homosexuals.

Lucifer had answered Yehuda's calls and visited the devastated man afterwards. He was heartbroken and he had cursed Lucifer. Lucifer should have punished Yehuda for this, as disrespecting an angel was a grave crime. But Lucifer chose to not punish the "old man". Fortunately, no outsiders witnessed Lucifer's failure to punish Yehuda, so there was no reason to escalate the matter.

Lucifer pitied Yehuda for his loss and Simon for the way he had died. Simon was a good kid, with his whole life ahead of him. Instead, he was punished with an excruciatingly painful death due to his sexual desires, something that was predetermined by his genes and not controllable from his end. Simon's punishment was very cruel considering he was unaware that he was committing a crime. Lucifer felt guilty for disregarding Simon's homosexuality as a non-issue when Yehuda had begged for his help, but there was nothing that Lucifer could have done about it.

The only "cure" for homosexuality was to change the genetic structure of the individual. This was incredibly difficult to do even on Earth and involved cryogenically freezing the individual to prevent cell death and then individually change every cell. Thus, it took years to alter the genome of an adult individual, and all genetic modification took place on embryos when it was easier to implant desirable human traits.

Lucifer had never understood other humans' obsession with sexuality. The angels had similar genetics when it came to sexuality; they were mostly asexual with a slight inclination towards heterosexuality. For as long as Lucifer had known Abraham, Abraham had not shown much interest in sex. But considering the amount of offspring Abraham had; this was probably age-related. Being 200 years younger than Abraham, Lucifer had never seen him before he started using DNA regenerating technology.

Lucifer was bothered that none of the other angels seemed to be disturbed by the events they had seen. Lucifer did not know whether his colleagues enjoyed taking part in atrocities or whether they feared Abraham's anger. Regardless, Lucifer needed to process what he had seen, but there was no one to talk to. He felt lonely and left out, and even considered leaving Eden and returning to Earth. But what would he do there? Lucifer had never been alone or outside his group of fellow angels. The fear of leaving it all behind was stronger than the fear of what he had become. Lucifer decided to sleep for a long time. The sleep would clear his mind, and the terrors he had seen, would seem less real once he woke up.

Chapter 49: Abraham Looks Ahead.

A few weeks later, a shipment of sexual inhibition medicine arrived, and Abraham instructed an angel to inject it straight into his brain. It caused a sharp pain as the drug was not meant to be administered that way, but the brain was the only part of Abraham's body that had survived. After the initial pain, Abraham felt a profound sense of relief as he could now think clearly without distractions and sexual desires. This enabled him to pursue more constructive goals. The burning of the sodomites made Abraham realise one thing. He now admitted to how much he enjoyed causing suffering and pain to others.

Abraham had never shunned from causing others pain, but he had always justified it with the greater good. He realised that this was because of morals imposed on him by others, but now there was no reason to be dishonest anymore. He had always liked torturing people and causing them pain. Strengthening Abraham's sadistic desires was the fact that he no longer had a human body and he was more machine than man. Before his heart and gut could feel compassion for others but with only the brain left, there was nothing that kept his sadism at bay.

Abraham considered torturing Lucifer for his disobedience. Abraham was aware of Lucifer's treacherous doubts in him. Had any other of the angels dared to question him like Lucifer, that angel would have been tortured and then murdered. But Lucifer was unique, he was created unique, and in this uniqueness laid the difficulty in making him succumb to Abraham's will.

Abraham had lost Lucifer once in the past and that was the darkest day of his life. He did not want to experience this again. Instead, Abraham aimed to form Lucifer in his image, and eventually hand over power to him whenever he was ready for final death.

Abraham felt the need to kill and torture someone. Although he did not need any reason to do so, he still preferred to make up a reason. Fortunately, it was a Saturday, and it was forbidden to work on Saturdays. Although someone always did work. Scanning through the minds of the Edenites he soon found his victim; a village healer who was treating a sick child. The village healer should have known better than doing his job on a Saturday! It was time to punish him.

Unfortunately, Lucifer was sleeping. Although this was for the best, as Abraham had decided against punishing Lucifer, who would object to the task at hand. Instead, he sent the angels Nuriel, Thomas and Michael to do his deed.

Michael who was third in command after Abraham and Lucifer approached the village healer and Abraham spoke through him:

- Greetings Mesaja.

- You are committing a great sin. Do you have anything to say for yourself?

Mesaja:

- Please forgive me, Master Michael. This child is ill and may not survive another day without help.

- I have worked hard to make life better for the villagers, and I try to honour Abraham's glory through my job.

Michael:

- And yet you didn't honour the holy day for him?

- If Grandmaster Abraham intends for this child to die; that is the way things should go.

- Since the child is sick on a Saturday, it is a sign to leave the child's fate into Abraham's hands.

- In his great mercy, Abraham will grant this child the gift of life while you shall suffer and die, for your sins.

Michael took out a vial of medication and injected it into the child. It was a fast-acting cure, and within minutes the child had recovered from his ailment. Michael spoke again:

- Behold people of Eden! Honour Abraham and pray for his mercy and he might grant it to you. Dishonour his glory and you shall suffer.

- Villagers, I'll leave it to you to carry out the punishment. Drag this wretched unbeliever to the village square and stone him to death.

Michael then injected Mesaja, with a stimulant that would keep him conscious for longer and increase his sensation of pain throughout the stoning. The villagers dragged Mesaja to the village square and they stoned him to death. Michael spoke again:

- Fantastic job, Edenites. You have proven your faithfulness to Abraham by killing this wretched man. Now tear his body into pieces and send to the other villages as a warning. No one disrespects Grandmaster Abraham unpunished!

When Michael returned to the Divine Control Center, Abraham congratulated him on a job well done. Not only had he shown that no one could break the holy laws in the Abrahameon but curing the child on the spot had proven that it was beneficial for the people of Eden to put their blind faith into the hands of Abraham.

Abraham would not often intervene and save sick children, because that would take away the miracle of the act and people would start expecting him to protect them. That idea was preposterous. They existed to please him and not the other way around. Then again, a miracle every now and then gave hope, and people that had hope for a better life were less likely to rebel, than individuals who had given up on hope and were ready to die.

Satisfied with the day's events Abraham went back to his throne room in the Divine Dimension. Abraham entered the trance-like state of meditation where he spent most of his time.

Chapter 50: The Selections Continue.

A few years later, Abraham awoke Lucifer from a session of cryogenic sleep. Lucifer felt confused and reckoned that Abraham must have stopped the cryogenic tank before the date it was programmed to.

Lucifer had felt very depressed the last decade, as he had lost his faith in Abraham's vision for Eden. Since he did not know what to do, he chose to sleep for months on end and only take part in special events and public holidays. Lucifer needed to talk to someone, but there was no one to speak to. If he spoke to Abraham about his concerns, he would be punished. If he spoke to the other angels, he would be met with disinterest, and if he was talking about his ethical issues with the Edenites, Abraham would him kill for exposing their lies.

Abraham contacted Lucifer:

- Wake up, Lucifer.
- You have a work obligation today.

Lucifer:

- Apologies, Master Abraham. But I cannot remember what that would be?

Abraham:

- Bah, all that extra sleep is bad for your brain. Today is the 1st of March, the first day of spring. You know what a new season means!

Lucifer:

But I thought the December girl was the 72nd offering, and that the debt with Ibrahim Rashid was settled?

Abraham:

- You are right, she was the 72nd, and the debt is paid.

- But I realised two things:

- Firstly: how do we stop the tradition? How do we tell the people of Eden that an appreciated and well-working tradition is no longer valid?

- Secondly: There is a fortune to be made in selling unregistered, healthy young virgin brides to wealthy buyers.

Lucifer:

- But I thought you had enough money to cover the upkeep of Eden?

Abraham:

- Don't be silly, Lucifer. There is no such thing as enough money in the world.

- I did not become the wealthiest man on Earth by limiting my vision.

Lucifer:

- Apologies, Grandmaster Abraham. I will gather a crew and do your bidding.

Lucifer was disappointed, but he refrained from saying anything. He could almost feel the pain in his head. The pain that Abraham had caused him throughout the years when Lucifer had disagreed with him. Lucifer felt old and he was indeed old, although he still looked like in his prime due to the time spent in cryogenic sleep and the massive usage of DNA regeneration technology.

Meanwhile, on Eden, a girl named Susanna planned to do something that had never happened before. She planned to volunteer to be selected. Technically, Susanna who was 14 years old and had reached puberty was not eligible. To be eligible one had to be a virgin and prepubescent. But Susanna was brave, inquisitive and she wanted to get away from Eden. Susanna wanted to leave because she was betrothed to a disgusting old man. She did not care that he was rich and would be able to support her and the many children to come. To multiply wasn't her life goal, and no matter what Abraham and Lucifer said, she would pursue her own independence.

Susanna had concluded the selected girls were not killed. She had seen many executions during her 14 years on Eden, but during the selection, the angels seemed very keen to not hurt the selected girl.

For this season's selection, Abraham chose a new approach. This time, he had set up an encrypted bidding platform where an auction took place. The girl that received the highest bid would be this season's selection.

Lucifer supervised the selection. He felt lacklustre and uninspired, but as the second in command of Eden he had to take part in the ceremony. Suddenly, Susanna walked up onto the podium where the young girls were displayed.

Lucifer:

- Stop!
- Step down from the podium woman, what is the meaning of this?

Susanna:

- I volunteer to be this season's selection.

Lucifer had a quick look a Susanna. He identified her as Susanna, and a brief moment later he had her biography uploaded into his brain.

Lucifer:

- Susanna, that is NOT how the selection works. The selection is not about volunteering; it's about being selected. Besides, you are not eligible.

Susanna:

- Eligible? I am a virgin, and I am sure that you know it, Lucifer.

Susanna's response baffled Lucifer. Usually, the Edenites were very respectful to him and his fellow angels. Sometimes people were begging and pleading to him which was difficult because Lucifer could not help everyone. With Susanna, things were different, she was breaking against convention by volunteering for the selection, and her tone of voice was sarcastic and mocking of Lucifer. Lucifer replied.

- You are not eligible because you have had your first bleeding.
- Now be gone, or I'll have you flogged

Susanna:

- Oh, come on, everyone knows what the selection is for. You must
be feeling lonely with no female angels up in your floating palace. I
am ready for you; these other girls are not.

Lucifer blushed. Despite living for almost 100 years, he had never been with a woman and he hadn't felt the urge to. As such he was not accustomed to this kind of language, and he hadn't heard anything like it since he left Earth 50 years earlier. He shouted back:

- That's enough!
- Guards, expel this woman and have her flogged!

Through a strange twist of fate, Susanna was saved. Mahmoud Rashid, Ibrahim's grandson, watched the auction and Susanna stole his heart. as she was beautiful and had a fiery personality. He placed a large bid for Susanna to save her life and make her his. As Abraham received the bid of 50 million Terran Credits, he commanded the angels to declare Susanna as the selection of the spring season.

Michael pushed Susanna into a portable cryogenic tank and flew back with her to the Divine Control Centre where she was shipped off to Mahmoud Rashid. Lucifer was stuck on Eden. He felt dumbfounded and speechless about what had happened. Eventually, he took off and left Eden for the Divine Control Center.

As for Susanna and Mahmoud, it was love at first sight. Although for Susanna the love was more based on the gratitude that Mahmoud paid a lot of money to have her taken off Eden, so she could experience all the wonders of the modern world and get away from Abraham's tyranny.

Unfortunately, their good times did not last long as Ibrahim Rashid was furious at his grandson for spending 50 million credits on a bride without his permission. The couple had to escape to Mars to avoid Ibrahim's wrath. Unfortunately, Mahmoud was weak and timid. He struggled to live on Mars and he perished after a decade

Susanna however, adapted to the times. Susanna's wits, intelligence and bravery made her a prominent smuggler and adventurer. She raised her and Mahmoud's daughter, whom she named Keila Eisenstein.

Chapter 51: Abraham Demands Sacrifices.

At the end of 2842, Abraham was crunching the numbers and calculating his total wealth and power. This year, the task that usually filled him with joy and bliss turned into anger and frustration. Looking back, he had been the wealthiest and most powerful, man in the solar system back in 2785 before he took upon himself to be Yahweh's successor

Back in 2785, Abraham had amassed the highest individual wealth ever known in the history of humanity. His influence had reached every nook and cranny of the solar system. His army had been the most efficient fighting force in the solar system due to their technological advantage. In 2842 his wealth was a fraction of what it had been and it totalled less than a billion Terran Credits. His reach and military might was non-existent outside of Eden. He felt like he had gone from a king to a chief tan of a small tribe living on a mostly empty and awfully expensive rock. The creation of Eden had totalled over 5 trillion Terran credits, and it was by far the costliest space colony ever built.

The reason Eden was so painfully expensive to create was because of the specifications Abraham chose for it. Eden was the most advanced space colony ever, and the first of its kind where someone could walk around with regular clothes and no technological aids whatsoever and still thrive. Another issue that drove up the cost was that all the machinery and technology that maintained Eden was hidden from the plain eye. Instead of having a visible water purification plant, Eden had an advanced chain of processing that replicated the water cycle from Earth with water evaporating and coming down as rain. The size of Eden also added to the costs. It would be much cheaper to terraform a smaller rock, but Abraham wanted to replicate Yahweh's work as closely as possible, so he picked an asteroid that replicated the size of the Holy Land. Adding to Abraham's woes, Eden did not produce anything of value, which could otherwise, had justified the cost. The Edenites were a bunch of freeloaders who did not appreciate Abraham's sacrifices for them. Abraham decided that the Edenites needed to make more sacrifices.

Abraham decided that those that benefitted the most from his rule were the ones who should make the sacrifice. This was not the angels as they had sacrificed a better life back on Earth for a life of celibacy and hardship helping him rule Eden. No, the real parasites were the high priests of each tribe! They benefitted from Abraham's reign as they were in positions of wealth and power based on his benevolence.

The population of Eden was divided into seven tribes although there was an 8th group of people that lived outside of the villages. Each of these tribes had a high priest that was appointed for life. While being appointed for life seemed helpful, it was a disadvantage as it meant an increased risk to be killed by Abraham from afar if he was dissatisfied with the high priest's performance. Once a high priest was dead the angels, would choose another villager to lead the town. Thus, the position of high priest was not hereditary although one could amass wealth for one's family that lasted after the high priest's death.

The Edenites gathered around Mount Sinai. The angels were dressed in their white ceremonial armours covered in gemstones. They were sparkling under the sun and the clear blue sky. Although people would die today, this was not a day of fear but a day to celebrate. Once they were all gathered, Lucifer spoke:

- Welcome Edenites, for our New Year's Eve celebration.

- Today we celebrate the year that has passed, and the year to come.

- But before we celebrate, I command all the high priests and their families to come up, as Grandmaster Abraham has an announcement to make.

While the high priests and their families were making their way up to the platform, the people were setting up the food and drink stations. The New Year celebration was a celebration of peace as the tribes were putting aside their differences for this celebration. The angels that supervised the celebrations made everyone think twice about causing any disturbances. Once the high priests were on the platform, they were all handed a glass of 'divine wine'. These were wines that had been bought from the finest wineries on Earth, which tasted better than the wines that the Edenites usually drank. The high priests praised the wine and wished everyone a happy new year to the sound of the cheering crowd. Suddenly, a hologram of Abraham appeared on top of the mountain.

Abraham:

- People of Eden. Happy New Year.

- I have a request for you.

- I request that your high priests make a sacrifice to honour my sacrifice.

- As you know the reason that you are living here in joy and happiness, is the sacrifice I made when I saved you from Yahweh's wrath. By protecting you, I gave up my place next to Yahweh in the spiritual afterlife.

- Instead, I am here, working tirelessly to support you by making it rain, making the air you breathe clean and making your crops grow. It is time for you to repay my sacrifice.

- High priests of Eden, you are the most fortunate of the Edenites. Today, I am giving you the opportunity to show your dedication and faith in me.

- At the altar, there is a sacrificial blade. Slit the throat of your first-born, and you shall be closer to my glory.

Among the high priests, was Yehuda, who had lost one of his daughters to the selection and one of his sons in the purges against homosexuals. Now he was to be tested again, and this time he was supposed to be the one carrying out the horrible deed. Yehuda made a choice; he would not let another one of his children die or disappear. It was the time to sacrifice his own life and say no to Abraham.

Yehuda:

- Grandmaster Abraham. I am grateful for your sacrifices, but I cannot do it. My children are everything to me, and I cannot bear the thought of losing another one before me. Take my life instead.

Before Abraham had the time to answer, Yehuda's oldest son, Jamal, spoke:

- Father, why are you doing this? You cannot deny Grandmaster Abraham his request.

- Abraham is the one granting us life. He deserves to decide when it is our time to go. I am honoured to die on his command.

Yehuda:

- But Jamal, your children are still young, they need you!

Jamal:

- My offspring will be fine. Grandmaster Abraham will look after them.

Having said this, Jamal walked up to the sacrificial altar. Yehuda walked after him slowly and with shaky legs. Yehuda cut Jamal's throat, and as the blood was pouring out of Jamal's dying body, Yehuda collapsed and started crying. Abraham spoke:

- Jamal set us an example for today. He will be granted a place in heaven for his will to give up his life to honour my name.

- I am asking the rest of the high priests to make the same sacrifice and do it gracefully and with joy in your hearts as thy firstborns will be granted a secure passage to heaven if you honour me.

The other high priests followed Abraham's command, and half an hour later the altar was covered in blood, with seven lifeless bodies next to it. Abraham spoke again:

- Rejoice Edenites, for tonight you have seen seven brave souls getting passage to heaven for their faith, dedication, and sacrifice.

- High priest Yehuda, you angered me by your lack of commitment, and the ungraceful way you dealt with Jamal's glorious sacrifice.

- I expel you and your family from the village. You must live in the wilderness near the edge of Eden without contact with other people. This is the only way your crime and debt can be repaid.

Yehuda, his five surviving children, and his grandchildren were gathered and led out in the desert by the angels Michael and Gabriel. They walked for many hours until they reached the edge of Eden, to a small cave facing the edge of space. Looking out one could only see the vast darkness of space. Michael injected Yehuda with a shot of DNA preserving serum. He spoke to the group.

- Family of Yehuda: This will be your new home. You're all cast out facing the abyss for the sins of your patriarch Yehuda, who dared to question Grandmaster Abraham.

- You shall live here, working twice as hard as the rest of your kind for half of the gain.

- Yehuda you shall face the biggest curse. You shall outlive all your children. Age and regret shall torment you, but you shall not die until Abraham lets you.

After saying this, Michael and Gabriel flew back to the Divine Control Centre and left the miserable Yehuda and his family cast out into the wilderness. In an act of desperation Yehuda leapt towards the edge of Eden to jump into the abyss. This failed as he collided with the nanotechnology layer that covered Eden. Yehuda was electrocuted and knocked unconscious. Once Yehuda woke up, he accepted his fate and he led his family's colonisation of this isolated part of Eden.

Chapter 52: Lucifer Falls from Above.

Lucifer felt demoralised and heartbroken. On Abraham's orders, he had conducted the latest atrocity against the Edenites. The victims were two young lovebirds who had gone against their families wishes and had rejected the arranged marriages their parents had organised so that they could be together.

With so many breaches against his divine law, Abraham wanted blood, and a public display. Lucifer was appointed to carry out the gruelling task. The young lovers had first had each fingernail pulled off one by one. They were then whipped with 50 lashes each. When Lucifer received the order to cut off the genitals of the victims with a rusty knife, he had enough. He pulled up his glowing plasma sword, the Dawn Bringer, and he decapitated the two lovers granting them a swift death.

Abraham was displeased but not furious with Lucifer. Abraham had opted to make this execution a display of Lucifer's power. Abraham sometimes sat back without showing himself to the Edenites and instead made it seem like the punishment was the will of a specific Angel. Lucifer was the figurehead while it was Abraham who pulled the strings speaking as a voice inside Lucifer's head. As Lucifer had not publicly disobeyed Abraham's orders, Abraham would not punish him.

Lucifer's plasma sword the, Dawn Bringer, was a modified version of the plasma knife that was standard equipment in the Terran military. It was a battery-powered device with a blade that could be superheated, and this way cut through any material with ease. A thin heat-resistant layer, that was held together by a magnetic field, covered the blade. This way the immense heat from the sword, did not spread to the surroundings but only to the parts cut, with surgical precision. While the Dawn Bringer was an impractical weapon, it looked impressive, and it spread fear and awe among the Edenites. As the Dawn

Bringer could cut through an angels' armour, it had a DNA activation technology that made Lucifer the only one who could wield it.

Lucifer decided to go back to the Divine Control Center. He would get scolded, and then he would get a few months of sleep. They were all going to sleep, as they were running low on medical supplies as well as spare parts for their angel suits. The shortage was because the infamous space pirate, Morgan Henry, had raided their latest shipment. It was not a big deal, space was vast, and the likelihood of facing space pirates was minimal.

Suddenly, Lucifer felt a collision and an electric shock. He realised that he had forgotten to open Eden's magnetic field and thus he had collided with it. The electric shock knocked him unconscious and he fell slowly to the ground.

Chapter 53: Lucifer Is Confused and Injured in the Wilderness.

Lucifer woke up. He was in pain and unable to move. His vision was blurry, and nothing made any sense to him. His head was pounding. Was he dead? Lucifer recalled that being cryogenically frozen was just like being dead, except that he wouldn't wake up from being dead. He was present and in pain hence he could not be dead but just injured. Lucifer tried to self-diagnose, he could wiggle his fingers and toes. Thus, his spine could not be broken, so why couldn't he get up?

Lucifer realised the answer. He couldn't get up because his armour was broken. Lucifer's angel suit was controlled by a chip in his brains and felt like a second skin, despite being heavy and requiring built-in motors to move. Thus, with the armour broken but that chip still active, Lucifer had believed that he was crippled when it was only his armour that broke. Lucifer got out of his angel armour.

Lucifer stood up, and for the first time in his life, he saw the world with his own eyes. Like the other members of the angel program, Lucifer had had a multitude of nanotechnology microchips inserted into his brain. These chips changed his perception of the world through enhancing colours, giving detailed information about every object, immediate facial recognition, his current location and his current objective, etc. Without the heightened perception of the world, Lucifer felt crippled. However, he also noticed something he had never felt before, he felt free, and he wanted to explore this brave new world.

But what would he do next? He was stuck in the wilderness, injured and thirsty. His freedom would be short-lived if he was to die out here. Lucifer was quite sure that the emergency beacon on his angel suit would still be functional. He could use it to get airlifted out to safety. Lucifer decided against activating the beacon. While it would save his life, it would also lead to the loss of his newfound freedom.

Lucifer looked around. He saw a hill in the distance and he decided to make his way there. From a hilltop, he would be able to scout the countryside and find a suitable place to find food and shelter. Securing a water supply was paramount, as he would not last long without it. He left his broken angel suit and most of his weapons. The weapons were too heavy and they had limited usefulness. Lucifer hoped that any human or animal he met had friendly intentions. It was pointless to resist if the Edenites were hostile towards him. Lucifer would rather die than take any more innocent lives. Lucifer opted to bring The Dawn Bringer sword, so that he could prove his identity.

Lucifer reached the hilltop and looked around for settlements and other points of interest. Lucifer felt that the angel chips in his brain was activated. Lucifer expected that Abraham had learned of his accident and was going to send help but instead something unexpected happened. Lucifer started seeing the world through Abraham's eyes. Lucifer understood that he was not meant to look at this, but he could not help himself. He needed to know about what was in Abraham's mind. He needed to see the truth to make sense of things.

What Lucifer saw shocked him. Things were not the way that Abraham had told him. Abraham had told Lucifer that Yahweh had met Abraham when Yahweh was on his deathbed. Yahweh had appointed Abraham to be his successor and create a new promised land called Eden. Lucifer had believed in this, and it had kept him going for all these years despite feeling that Abraham's action was wrong and evil.

Lucifer saw the truth. Yahweh was one out of many extra-terrestrials that had used superior technology to manipulate humans into believing he was a god. He had done so, to make them fight his wars. Yahweh was never interested in humanity's happiness; he had only aimed to use and exploit them. Lucifer realised that Abraham had done the same thing, and that he was an accomplice in Abraham's atrocities. Lucifer felt a sickened realising what he had done, but the worst part was when he had a glimpse into Abraham's soul. There was nothing but anger, contempt and insatiable lust for power and control. Abraham did not keep the people Eden alive because he loved them but only because he needed them to fulfil his desire for power. Injured from the electric shock and the fall Lucifer passed out again.

Chapter 54: A Wounded Stranger in the Wilderness.

The siblings Sara and John were foraging in the wilderness when they came across the injured Lucifer. They did not recognise him. He was wearing a blue tracksuit covered in blood and he did not look like the archangel without his angel armour. They were scared and did not know what to do. The Abrahameon did not mention what to do when one came across an injured stranger in the desert. Regardless of what they did, their tyrannical Grandmaster Abraham, could find a reason to punish them.

They had experienced this irrational vengefulness when their uncle Simon was tortured and killed because he was a homosexual. Back then, homosexuality was not a sin, but Abraham had insisted that Simon should have understood that it was a sinful act. The reason that they lived in isolation at the fringe of Eden was that their grandfather, Yehuda, had shown reluctance to sacrifice their other uncle Jamal. Eventually, Sara decided that they should try to save the stranger. She told her brother to go home and get some help.

Sara had a closer look at the wounded stranger. He looked familiar, like one of the angels. She could not tell for sure since she rarely saw the angels. The wounded man was handsome, way better looking than any of the men in her household. She felt a bit of shame, as lust was a sin and sin had destroyed humanity's homeworld and condemned the few survivors to Eden. Copulation was essential for the survival of the species, but it should only happen within the wedlock, and she shouldn't yearn for it. The Abrahameon was very particular of this. The fact that it was forbidden to crave sex, made Sara want it more. She went down on her knees and she started dressing Lucifer's wounds. Sara got startled when Lucifer opened his eyes.

Lucifer was confused when he woke up. He couldn't remember where he was or how he had got there. He could not check his vitals, as all the chips in his brain were broken. He looked to his side, and he saw a beautiful woman sitting next to him. Dead or not dead, he was not in hell. Lucifer spoke:

- Am I dead? Are you an angel?

Sara:

- Don't be silly; all the angels on Eden are men.
- You look familiar, are you an angel.

Lucifer:

- I don't know; I used to be.

Sara:

- What happened?

Lucifer:

- I fell.

Sara:

- I understand

Neither of them said anything else. There was no need to say anything. They were enchanted by each other. For Lucifer, it was the first time that he saw the world with his own eyes, and Sara was the most beautiful woman he had ever seen.

Because of his implants, Lucifer had never appreciated beautiful women and never had any interest in sex. He could feel his desire towards Sara, but he had no energy to pursue it, so they both sat there in silence enchanted by each other. Eventually, John came back with his horse cart and brought the wounded Lucifer back to his house where Sara nursed him back to health. When Lucifer recovered, he and Sara had each other, over and over, their desire for each other was overwhelming.

Chapter 55: Yehuda's Dilemma.

Due to the DNA Regeneration technology that he was exposed to a decade earlier Yehuda had reached the age of 80, and he had witnessed the death of all his children. Seeing the death of all his children had not left him lonely and miserable as he had a dozen grandchildren ranging in age between 20-40 years old, to look after.

Lucifer had not waited long before fornicating with Yehuda's granddaughter, Sara. After that, he had asked Yehuda for Sara's hand in marriage. Since they had already fornicated, it was a mortal sin for them not to get married. But Yehuda did not know why Lucifer fell and what would happen if the former angel stayed with his family. He decided to discuss the matter with Lucifer.

Yehuda:

- Lucifer, why are you here, why did you fall from heaven?

Lucifer:

- Call me Terrence. Lucifer is my employee name, and I am no longer working for Abraham Goldstein.

Yehuda:

- Okay Terrence. Why did you fall from heaven?

Lucifer

- I forgot to deactivate the electromagnetic field surrounding Eden and I got electrocuted. The collision broke my equipment, I passed out, and I crashed onto the surface of Eden.

Yehuda:

- Nothing of this makes any sense. You look like Lucifer, but you don't act like Lucifer. If it weren't for your eyes, I would take you for an imposter.

Lucifer had luminescent blue eyes. Having glowing eyes was a fashion trend for newborn babies on Earth the previous century. Mixing the human eye colour DNA with DNA from animals with luminous eyes created glowing eyes in humans. It did not noticeably change an individual's vision, and Lucifer's enhanced eyesight had been dependent on implanted microchips that allowed him to see the ultraviolet and the infrared part of the spectrum.

Lucifer decided to come clean and expose the truth to Yehuda. There was no reason to lie, and Lucifer was a doomed man regardless of what he did. Lucifer knew that Abraham would not be merciful to him this time. It didn't matter. Lucifer accepted his fate, and his only regret was that he had helped Abraham's atrocities.

Although, Lucifer had questioned Abraham at times, he had never tried to stop him. Instead, he had kept his doubts to himself and carried out his duties. The accident had changed everything. When his bionic microchips broke, Lucifer experienced what it felt like to be human for the first time; to love and be loved.

Yehuda:

- So, you are saying that Earth is still around? That we are living in the future and that Eden is a deception by an evil madman?

Lucifer:

- You could sum it up like that.

Yehuda:

- It sounds crazy, but I believe you, Lucifer.
- So, how do we stop Abraham's tyranny and win our freedom?

Lucifer:

- We cannot stop Abraham, that's impossible.

Yehuda:

- If Abraham and the angels are humans, then they can be stopped.

Lucifer:

- Yehuda, you don't understand. Abraham can read your mind and kill you at any time via the microchip in your brain. If he couldn't do that, he could destroy all life on Eden by turning off the electromagnetic field that keeps the atmosphere in place. Resistance to him is futile.

Yehuda:

- He can kill me if he wishes. I would welcome my death. Abraham killed several of my children, and then he extended my life so that I would see my other children die of natural causes. I am ready to die for a worthy cause.

Lucifer:

- Well, I am over a century old, so I guess I am ready to go as well.
- What do you suggest?

Yehuda:

- You need to make me untraceable to Abraham and the other angels. These microchips that you are talking about; can I remove them?

Lucifer:

- I always thought they were irremovable. But the accident proved that they can be deactivated through using the electromagnetic field surrounding Eden.

Yehuda:

- Excellent. I know what you are talking about. I tried to jump off the edge of Eden when Abraham condemned me. I experienced excruciating pain and I woke up feeling burnt.

Lucifer:

- Yes, you were lucky to survive.

Yehuda:

- A blessing and a curse! Anyways, can you help this old man win his freedom?

Lucifer:

- I believe that I can Yehuda. Keep in mind, if I am wrong, you'll die.

Yehuda:

- That's a risk that I am willing to take. Let's go.

Lucifer and Yehuda walked to where Lucifer had left his broken angel suit. Once Lucifer had found the broken angel armour, he took the parts needed to deactivate Yehuda's chip. Lucifer cut off some electrical cables, and he also took one of the gloves to insulate. Unwittingly, while helping Lucifer to gather the parts, Yehuda activated the silent emergency switch on Lucifer's armour alerting Abraham that Lucifer was in danger.

Lucifer and Yehuda headed towards the edge of Eden. Once they reached the edge, Lucifer connected one part of the electrical cord to Yehuda's ear. This was close to where Yehuda's human chip was attached to his brain stem. Lucifer put on the insulating glove and led the cable to the electromagnetic field covering Eden. Yehuda emitted a sharp scream before passing out. Lucifer hesitated for a second. He did not know if he had killed Yehuda or if everything was going according to plan.

Lucifer pulled out the Dawn Bringer, cut an opening in Yehuda's skull, and removed the chip. Lucifer felt observed and he turned around. He saw a group of angels lead by Michael.

Michael:

- What are you doing, Lucifer?

- You destroyed your suit; you weren't waiting for emergency pick up, and instead you killed this old man here at the edge of Eden. Explain yourself.

Lucifer felt paralysed and was out of words. If they knew what he had done he would face the death penalty for treason. But they did not know. Lucifer's microchips were fried, and Yehuda was most likely dead and would not expose him.

Michael:

- Answer me, Lucifer!

Lucifer decided to fake amnesia and replied:

- Lucifer who is that? I am Terrence Lowenstein. I am a Terran Citizen and senior security operative for House Goldstein. Who are you?

Michael signalled Nuriel, who shot Lucifer with a tranquiliser dart. They put Lucifer put in a life support unit, and they travelled back to the Divine Control Center.

Chapter 56: Abraham Doubts Lucifer and Decides His Fate.

Abraham observed Lucifer who lay unconscious on an operation table. Abraham wondered what Lucifer had been up to for the last two weeks. He damned himself for not noticing that Lucifer was missing. The mistake was an unfortunate consequence of the way they were running Eden. The angels were cryogenically frozen for extended periods, to expand their lifespans. When Lucifer disappeared, he was the only angel on active duty, and no one had noticed that he was gone. Abraham should have seen it, but he was meditating in the Divine Dimension and had not conveyed Lucifer any thoughts. Abraham hadn't given Lucifer any attention as Lucifer's angel chip malfunctioned and showed that it was active when it was broken.

So, how had this happened? Had Lucifer destroyed his angel suit and chip or was it an accident? Abraham wanted to believe that it was an accident, but the facts did not add up. If it was an accident, Lucifer would have activated the emergency beacon straight away. But if Lucifer had betrayed him, why had he destroyed his uniform and stayed on Eden, when it made more sense trying to kill Abraham.

Michael claimed that Lucifer had acted strange when the angels found him. For unclear reasons, Lucifer had killed Yehuda at the edge of Eden. Lucifer had acted as if he had severe amnesia. He had stated his Terran name and title despite not using either for the last 60 years. It was unlikely that Lucifer had amnesia that made him forget the previous 60 years of his life, but Abraham could not rule out the possibility. It was possible, that Lucifer, being controlled via the Angel chip, had not accumulated any biological memories. This would lead to complete amnesia if the angel chip broke.

Abraham decided to figure out what Lucifer did on Eden in the weeks between the destruction of his angel suit, and the activation of the emergency beacon. Lucifer must have gotten outside help; otherwise, he would have died from starvation or dehydration. This was easy to investigate, as there was only the Yehuda family in the vicinity of the crash site.

A few minutes later, Abraham was furious. Lucifer had misbehaved and spent the last weeks copulating and getting emotionally attached to a young woman called Sara. Sexual activity outside of marriage was forbidden and Lucifer could not get married, as Abraham would never allow it. The Angels existed to serve Abraham and they should keep away from other distractions. A worse crime than the premarital coitus was that Lucifer had proven to be just a man. The Yehuda family had seen him without his technology, and they would conclude that the other angels were also ordinary men with technology. If this rumour were to spread, Abraham's control over Eden would fail, as its inhabitants would realise that he was their captor and not their god. The Edenites couldn't find out the truth, and Abraham had to eliminate the Yehuda family.

Abraham needed to kill Lucifer, but he hesitated. Lucifer was unique compared to the other angels. The other angels had their human DNA created from scratch with specific abilities chosen for them and designed for specific tasks. They had then been put in a synthetic womb and created with no human involvement attached. This was a highly illegal practice as the creations were beings without souls and free will. Combined with specific implants that enhanced their abilities and controlled their behaviour Abraham had created a proficient group of operatives that had no other desires in life than to serve Abraham. The other angels, were just efficient machines to Abraham and if one malfunctioned, he would dispose of that angel.

Lucifer was different. His DNA wasn't created from scratch; instead, Abraham had based Lucifer on someone that Abraham held very dear. Furthermore, he was born by a surrogate mother instead of a synthetic womb, so he had a soul and a free will. Abraham had been able to control most of Lucifer's mind with the angel chip, but in the end, he still had an underlying personality. Lucifer's character was an essential aspect, as Abraham sought Lucifer's approval, whom he had created to be his heir.

Abraham decided to give Lucifer one more chance to live and be his heir. To get this opportunity, Lucifer would have to make a sacrifice. He would have to kill Sara, and her family to show his dedication to Abraham. If Lucifer passed this trial, he would regain his place. If he failed, he would die, and he would have given up his life for nothing. Abraham decided to cryogenically freeze Lucifer and then fix him once a shipment with all his implants arrived. Lucifer would have the choice to obey or die, but Abraham wanted to make sure that Lucifer chose to follow. To replace Lucifer's broken implants and microchips was the best way to achieve this.

Having decided this, Abraham went to the Divine Dimension to meditate.

Chapter 57: Yehuda Survives and Desires Revenge.

Yehuda woke up a couple of hours later. It was a painful and strange awakening for Yehuda. He could no longer feel Abraham's presence and instead he was looking out in the blackness of space with no gods to worship. He recognised this feeling from his youth when he visited many asteroids like Eden. Yehuda got up on his feet. He saw the golden microchip, soaked in blood, that Lucifer had extracted from his head. He knew what it was; he had seen similar microchips in his past.

Yehuda saw details in the landscape that he had never noticed before. It was technology instead of magic, but he was still fascinated by it. He could see the exhaust pipes extracting fresh oxygen from the core of Eden. Yehuda could see how six out of Eden's seven suns were glimmering, indicating that they were satellites reflecting the sun's light while the seventh celestial object that wasn't blinking was the actual sun. From the size of the sun, he deduced that he was somewhere in the Asteroid belt 50 % further away from the sun than his home planet Mars.

While Yehuda was impressed by his sudden mental clarity, he had a more pressing matter at hand. He was injured, and his mind was too muddled to find the way home in this featureless landscape. Fortunately, his grandchildren Sara and John had set out to look for him, and with the aid of the family dog, they found him.

Sara:

- Grandfather! I heard that you and Lucifer set out to discuss something.
- You are bleeding, what happened?

Yehuda:

- Lucifer did this to me.
- He left me for dead and took off

Sara:

- That's impossible! He loved me. He was going to ask you for permission to marry me.

Yehuda:

- He was a fallen angel. The worst of sinners condemned by his Master.

Sara:

- That means nothing. Abraham condemned us and we are still good people

- Lucifer was a tormented soul, plagued by the pain he had caused others. That's why he wanted to change. That was why he loved me.

Yehuda:

- That's enough, woman! Show some respect!
- Lucifer is gone, and he won't be back
- John, I command you to take me home and treat my wounds.

Hearing this, John rushed up to Yehuda, bandaged him, and carried the old man back to safety, while Sara stayed behind wailing out her misery.

A few days later, Yehuda had recovered, and he made up his mind. He would not tell his grandchildren the truth about Eden. They were born on Eden, and for them, it was the only truth. Besides he would put them in grave danger if he told them the truth. The villain posing as Grandmaster Abraham, the almighty god of Eden, could still read their minds through the microchips in their heads. If Yehuda told them the truth, he would put them in danger. Yehuda could not remove the chip from his grandchildren's heads, as he lacked the skill and know-how to carry out the operation. Yehuda bit his lip and swore to himself: *"He would make Abraham pay."*

Chapter 58: Yehuda Finds Out That Sara is Pregnant.

Three months later, Yehuda discovered that Sara was pregnant. His earlier religious self would have condemned this, but having regained most of his memories, he no longer had any strong opinions about extramarital conceptions.

Yehuda no longer feared the "god" Abraham although he still feared the villain Abraham. Yehuda wondered when Abraham's "angels" would show up to punish his family for siding with a fallen angel.

Yehuda remembered his life before Eden. Yehuda's family were a prominent family living in relative wealth until a Martian warlord invaded his city. Rather than staying under the new ruler's tyranny, Yehuda's family had fled to Earth. They knew that Martians were not allowed on Earth. However, vast areas of Earth consisted of depopulated national parks where a family could survive undetected.

Terran border patrols captured Yehuda's family, and they were locked up in the gruesome Kaguya Detention Centre on the Moon. They had volunteered to join the Eden expedition, but for some reason, Yehuda was paired up with a new woman when he woke up on Eden. Since they had lost their memories neither of them was able to see through the deception. Yehuda was certain that he never had seen the rest of his original family on Eden and he concluded that Abraham must have killed them. Yehuda realised that Grand Master Abraham was Abraham Goldstein, as House Goldstein had funded the Eden Project.

Yehuda wanted to expose Abraham, but he didn't know how. If he told people the truth, they wouldn't believe him, and Abraham would come after him.

Yehuda needed a long-term plan to overthrow Abraham, and he found a viable solution. Under the surface of Eden, there were widespread maintenance tunnels. These tunnels were ideal for growing mushrooms. If Yehuda could farm enough mushrooms, he could feed the people that he freed from Abraham while being undetectable from orbit. It was a long shot, but it was his best option to start with. Besides, Yehuda had time. The life-extending vaccine that the angels had given him as a punishment, would turn against them. Once he could farm enough mushrooms, he would free his family to start the rebellion. It would be a slow-moving underground movement, but it would work, and Abraham would face justice for his crimes.

Chapter 59: A child is born.

Today a child was born in the Terran star system. This is a unique child with psionic capabilities that only happens once in every 20 billion individuals. Since the last person who possessed these skills did not serve us as we hoped, this child must be guided and supervised to make her stay on the path. Since humanity now has the technology needed for our return, this individual can be our saviour.

Unknown source on the 22nd of March 2850 A.D

Chapter 60: Lucifer Faces an Ultimatum.

Lucifer woke up in the medical ward and he felt strange. All his auxiliary system was running, and his vision was once again amplified and high-lighting detailed information about the surroundings. Worse yet, Abraham had fixed his angel chip and could read his thoughts again. Lucifer wondered if his memories from Eden was just a dream.

Lucifer didn't understand why Abraham hadn't wiped his memories. If Abraham did not intend to kill him for treason, why did he remember about his actions? Lucifer noticed that he was strapped to a bed. Abraham walked in followed by a group of angels.

Abraham walked up to Lucifer and studied him. After a moment of silence, he spoke:

- Lucifer, do you know why you are here? Do you remember what sins you committed?

Lucifer nodded but said nothing.
Abraham spoke again:

- You are here because you betrayed me. Your lists of sins are endless and yet you are still alive.

- You see, I am a benevolent leader.

- You have freedom as long as you follow my rules. Yet, you cannot live up to my standards.

Lucifer:

- Freedom? I have been stuck on this rock for 60 years doing your will. I have put innocents through trials and torment

Abraham:

- Yet you never left. I never said that you could not abandon my service. You are just my employee.

Lucifer:

- I did not know what I would do with my life.

Abraham:

- You see, that is your problem. You have freedom to do things, and yet you don't. When you chose to do something, you want the wrong thing.

- When you chose to copulate with Sara, you didn't think. By following your basic instinct to procreate you made her a sinner and you signed her death warrant.

Lucifer:

- I don't know what happened. I couldn't resist the urge. I love her.

Abraham:

- If you had loved her, you would have watched over her as an angel. She would have lived a good life. Instead, she will die, because of you.

Lucifer:

- No, it is your laws that condemn and kill people. I believe in love and freedom.

Abraham:

- Funny that you say that.

- Martians are free. They are impulse-driven, they copulate based on desire instead of logic, and they don't control their population growth. Consequently, Mars is a wasteland with 4 billion individuals fighting for limited resources due to inability to put society ahead of individual needs.

- On Earth only the wealthy or people with exceptional genes are allowed to procreate. As a result, Earth has a sustainable population and a healthy thriving society.

Lucifer:

- On Earth, you have a plutocracy that is bleeding the solar system dry.

Abraham:

- Yet every obedient Terran citizen enjoys a wealthy and safe life. Living this way is worth more than the notion of "freedom."

- The Edenites are lucky. I rescued them from a terrible detention centre and I put them on the most advanced terraformed asteroid ever built.

- Eden is disease free, and if they work hard and follow the rules, they will live good lives.

Lucifer:

- You call public executions, floggings and torture a good life with benevolent leadership? You are insane!

Abraham struck Lucifer with a psionic blast. Lucifer was writhing in pain and almost passed out before Abraham released the pressure.
Abraham:

- Silence you fool. I am doing it for the people. I could kill any undesirables through the divine technology chip.

- Yet, I don't. Instead, I make a public example of the worst sinners to
teach the others the proper way to live. I am showing them the way
to a long happy life instead of the misery that comes from following
primitive impulses.

Lucifer looked at Abraham in disgust and said nothing. It surprised Lucifer
that Abraham was so outspoken about his villainy in front of the other angels.
Abraham spoke again

- The other angels disapprove of the mercy that I am showing you.

- But I love you like a son and it is difficult for me to give you the
punishment that you deserve.

- But you need to feel the pain that your actions have caused me.

- Your whore, Sara, gave birth today. She and the child are a product
of sin, and they must be purged. If you purge them, I will forgive
your sins, and you'll retake your rightful place. If you refuse, you'll
die.

Lucifer:

- But she is innocent, you monster!

Abraham:

- No, she is not. She knew that fornicating with you was a sin and
she still did it. She defied my will multiple times. She gave in to her
primitive impulses instead of trusting my divine plan. Her life is lost.
Your life is your choice.

Lucifer was shaking with anger and he didn't know what to do. Abraham
had shown his true self, and Lucifer's regretted helping this evil for so many

years. He wanted to tell Abraham to go fuck himself, but that would not save Sara. Lucifer did not care about his own life, but he had to save Sara and his child. Eventually, Lucifer spoke:

- Master Abraham, you are right. Forgive me for doubting your divine will and wisdom. I will carry out the task to redeem myself.

Abraham:

- Very well.

- I will leave you so that you can prepare. Do not even think about betraying me.

As Abraham and the angels left the room, Michael spoke to Abraham:

- Grandmaster Abraham, I don't like this. He will betray us again.

Abraham:

- Perhaps. But I have reasons for giving Lucifer a final chance to redeem himself.

- Just trust in my judgment and be loyal, Michael.

Michael:

- Understood, Grandmaster!

Abraham:

- Go to Eden and be within striking distance from Lucifer. Smite him if he betrays us.

Chapter 61: Lucifer Rebels.

Yehuda saw Lucifer approaching, and he felt that his greatest fear was about to happen. Yehuda had been surprised by the lack of intervention from Abraham and he had hoped that his family's aid towards Lucifer had gone unnoticed.

When Yehuda found out that Sara was pregnant, he concluded that Abraham would wait until the child was born terrorise the family by killing the child. Lucifer's return confirmed this suspicion. Yehuda didn't waste any time. He ran into the bedchamber where Sara was resting. She had given birth to non-identical twins, a boy and a girl. The girl looked like her mother and most Edenites with brown eyes, dark hair, and olive skin. The boy looked like Lucifer with his straight blonde hair and his dad's most prominent feature, the blue luminescent eyes.

That Sara had given birth to twins was a blessing and a curse. The blessing was that Yehuda could take one of the children away without Abraham noticing. The sad part was that the one he left behind would probably be killed. Yehuda chose to take the boy. The son of Lucifer could be a crucial ingredient in a future rebellion and his resemblance to Lucifer was so apparent so people wouldn't disregard this claim. Yehuda grabbed the baby boy and ran to the ventilation tunnels where he was cultivating mushrooms.

Lucifer stormed into the room where Sara was resting. He shouted to wake her up

- Sara, we need to go, there is not much time.

Sara was confused to see Lucifer after such a long time. His tense voice made it clear that this was not a social visit.

Sara:

- What's happening Terrence? Where have you been? You left without a word.

Lucifer:

- Sara, you are in danger. Abraham wants me to kill you.
- I am here to save you, and I need to get you to safety.

Sara:

- But what did I do wrong?

Lucifer:

- You did not do anything wrong, Sara.
- However, we both sinned when we had sex before marriage.
- Let's grab the child and run away.

Sara:

- Children, there is a boy and a girl.

Lucifer:

- No, there is only one. Hurry up! Follow me!

Lucifer grabbed the baby girl and Sara ran after him. They ran towards the force field at the edge of Eden. They reached the place where Lucifer had freed Yehuda, nine months earlier. The electrical cable that Lucifer had used to release Yehuda was still there. Lucifer turned to Sara and spoke.

- Sara, do you trust me?

Sara:

- What is happening? Why are we at the edge of the world?

Lucifer:

- This will hurt a lot, but after that, you'll be free. And I can bring you to safety.

- Are you ready?

Sara:

- Yes, Terrence.
- ... I love you.

Lucifer did not answer. Instead, he electrocuted Sara to deactivate the chip. He used a scalpel sized plasma knife to make a cut in Sara skull and take out the microchip. Lucifer then sealed her wound and gave her a shot of a fast-acting stimulant to bring her back to consciousness. He looked around and realised that he was surrounded and frozen in place. A group of angels led by Michael and Gabriel approached him.
Michael:

- Lucifer, you traitor!

- Your betrayal does not stop at fucking these people. You are even stealing them from their master.

Lucifer:

- I am setting them free. She is innocent!
- Kill me if you must.

Michael:

- Yes, you'll die. But so must your whore.
- You could have given her a swift death and redeemed yourself.
- Instead, you chose to cause her a painful death and doomed your-self
- I'll make you watch her die.

Gabriel grabbed Sara while Michael pulled up a rusty knife and cut off pieces from Sara's body. Her tormented screams built up agony and wrath within Lucifer who was stuck in place. Lucifer was unable to move as Abraham controlled him like a puppet.

Lucifer closed his eyes. He could feel it. It grew stronger and stronger and he could see it. He could sense the signal that Abraham used to keep him in place. He mustered his mental strength and reversed the signal. Then he knocked Abraham unconscious with a psionic blast. Lucifer was free to move. He moved quickly, and stabbed Michael with his plasma knife. He then shoved Gabriel to free Sara. Lucifer did not get far. Weakened by the mental battle with Abraham, he had no chance to avoid the rain of bullets fired by the angels. Multiple rounds hit Lucifer and Sara; Sara died on the spot while Lucifer was crippled and mortally wounded. With his dying breaths, Lucifer crawled to Michael and savaged his body with the plasma knife to prevent resurrection. Having done this, he turned around, looked at the sky and took his last breath.

Gabriel got up and he witnessed the carnage. He was now the highest ranked angel. He had not imagined that the day would end like this. Abraham had given Lucifer an undeserved chance to redeem himself by killing the vile temptress. Instead, the witch had cast a spell on Lucifer turning him against his brothers.

Gabriel did not understand why so many humans were obsessed with the sin of the flesh and he had never imagined that Lucifer would fall for it. Gabriel contacted Abraham who had regained consciousness from the psionic blast.

Gabriel:

- Lucifer killed Michael. We had to kill Lucifer as a response. Lucifer's vile temptress is also dead.

Abraham:

- What about the baby girl?

Gabriel looked around and he found the baby girl wrapped in a blanket clutched to her dead mother's chest. Miraculously, the baby was unharmed.

Gabriel:

- The baby is unharmed.

Abraham:

- Excellent. Bring the baby and the bodies of Lucifer and Michael back to me. Leave the corpse of the woman; she can rot there as a warning.

Gabriel:

- Affirmative.
- Master Abraham. How could Lucifer move? I thought you restrained him?

Abraham:

- I... I don't know.

Chapter 62: Abraham's Woes Before Lucifer's Execution.

Abraham felt grief. He had offered to pardon Lucifer, and Lucifer had met his leniency with disloyalty. Abraham could not give Lucifer another chance after this, and he regretted his course of action. If he could go back in time, he would have memory-wiped Lucifer, and everything would be okay.

But erasing Lucifer's memory was never an option for Abraham. He wanted Lucifer to obey him by his own free will. Abraham looked at Lucifer's dead body. He recalled the fate of his firstborn son, Terrence Goldstein, who had died 200 years earlier.

Abraham and Terrence had been on a business meeting in Sydney. Back then they were just a regular sized company and not the wealthiest and most powerful faction on the planet. As they left the office, assassins drove past them and shot at them from a passing car. Abraham pulled Terrence in front of him, and used him as a human shield. When the assailants drove off, Terrence was dead and beyond resurrection. Abraham's spirit had died on that fateful day. Filled with remorse and anger, he could no longer relate to feelings like joy and love. Instead, he became very cynical widening the gap to his wife and his children. With his increased cynicism he could focus on his new goal, to maximise his wealth and power.

Lucifer was different from the other angels as he was a modified clone of Terrence Goldstein. Abraham had never told him the truth. He had told Lucifer that he was an orphan who was admitted to the ANGEL program as he had extraordinary genes. Abraham had hidden Lucifer's real identity to protect him from other relatives within House Goldstein and to give him a better upbringing. Abraham knew that growing up in excessive wealth corrupted individuals and Abraham wanted Terrence to be the best he could be.

Despite Lucifer being his secret son, Abraham could not save his life anymore. He had stepped over a line when he killed Michael to save Sara. Abraham knew that discontentment among the angels, would spread if he spared Lucifer. The angels were furious over the death of Michael who had been their de-facto leader as Lucifer was too unlike the other angels to lead them.

Abraham studied Lucifer's and Michael's dead bodies. It was still possible to resurrect Lucifer, while Michael was beyond repair. With the available technology, it was usually possible to resurrect someone unless the brain was destroyed. Most body parts could be grown from stem cells, but a destroyed brain could not be regrown from scratch. This was because all the information in the brain would be lost, and a stem-cell grown brain, would be as developed as the brain of a newborn baby.

Abraham made his choice. The angels wanted for blood, and they should have it. It would take a couple of weeks to regrow Lucifer's damaged body parts and resurrect him. Abraham told Gabriel, who was the new archangel, what do.

Abraham thought about Lucifer's baby daughter, who was Abraham's granddaughter. She looked so small and gentle where she lay, and Abraham gave her the name Adina. Adina was the best of two worlds. Genetically she was a mix of the perfect genetics created with Terran technology and the natural selection of the Edenites.

Abraham wanted to see his granddaughter growing up, so he inserted an angel chip into Adina's brain so that he would get a stronger connection with her. He searched for suitable foster parents and Abraham discovered that High Priest Markus' wife had recently given birth and could breastfeed Adina as well. He instructed Gabriel to present Adina to Markus and make sure that he took proper care of the child.

After this, Abraham transported his mind to the Divine Dimension and entered a deep meditative trance. Lucifer's execution would be a gruesome affair, and Abraham wanted nothing to do with it!

Chapter 63: Lucifer's Execution.

A few weeks later, Gabriel resurrected Lucifer for the execution. Much to Gabriel's dismay, Abraham was in deep meditation and ignored him, so the angels had to execute Lucifer without Abraham's supervision. Gabriel ordered the Edenites to gather at Mount Sinai for an important message. The angels dressed up in their white angel armour to symbolise that they came to enlighten the people and bring peace and wisdom. Lucifer was brought down in chains.

The crowd gathered in anticipation. Usually, important gatherings started with Abraham giving a speech. But today his absence was notable, with the crowds murmuring and Gabriel felt a bit reluctant. Eventually, he spoke:

- People of Eden

- We are here today to prove that no one stands above the law, not even the former Archangel Lucifer.

Lucifer screamed out in his defence, but his voice was not amplified, so the people couldn't hear him. Gabriel ended Lucifer's slur with a punch to the face that knocked him to the ground.
Gabriel:

- Like I said, not even Lucifer stands above the law.

- Three weeks ago, he was caught fornicating with an Edenite woman and he tried to persuade her to turn against Grandmaster Abraham.

- When the angel Michael sought to bring Lucifer back to heaven, Lucifer stabbed him in the head with a magical knife strong enough to kill an angel.

- For these great crimes, Grandmaster Abraham stripped Lucifer of his immortality. Today, we will witness Lucifer purged from sin, so his dark soul can reach the afterlife.

- Let the proceedings begin

The execution of Lucifer was the most brutal display ever performed on Eden. The 24 angels, enraged by the loss of Michael, each subjected Lucifer to their gruelling choice of torture. Lucifer's heart stopped a dozen times, and he was revived each time to continue the pain and extend his suffering. After eight hours of continuous torture, Gabriel was satisfied and he used an orbital laser to vaporise Lucifer. The angels then took off and left.

The execution of Lucifer did not have the effect that the angels and Abraham had hoped for. Lucifer was the most loved angel among the Edenites, and he became a symbol of love and freedom. An underground cult arose around Lucifer in the decades that followed the execution.

Chapter 64: Yehuda Finds a Foster Family for Jeshua.

When he saw Lucifer approaching, Yehuda had grabbed Lucifer's baby son and he went into hiding. He had escaped unnoticed, but as he held the infant boy in his hands, he realised that he had a problem. A baby could not live off the mushrooms, that he grew in these tunnels.

Fortunately, Yehuda had come across several suitable foster families during his travels on Eden. He concluded that the best option would be to leave the child in the care of the couple Akiva and Chana who had young children that Chana still breastfed.

Yehuda told Akiva that Jeshua was already baptised and that both parents had died of illness. Akiva believed in Yehuda's story and he agreed to raise Jeshua as his son.

After leaving Jeshua in the care of Akiva and Chana, Yehuda returned to the tunnels where he planned his rebellion. Suddenly, he felt weary and his body ached. He found a reflective surface and he watched his reflection. Yehuda realised that he had aged a lot since. His rapid aging meant that the anti-aging vaccine that Michael had injected him with, had stopped working.

Yehuda knew that unless he injected a new dosage of DNA regeneration technology, he would age quickly and die soon. This realisation came as a blessing and curse for Yehuda. He had wanted to die for a long time, but now that he had a purpose to live, his time was up. Not wanting to fight his fate, Yehuda smoked some herbs, fell asleep, and died peacefully in his sleep.

Chapter 65: Adina Realises That She is Special.

The first five years of Adina's life was unremarkable. As a small child the angel chip had no discernible effect on her. When she turned five, she realised that she was special.

The first clue was that her parents could not tell whether they were her parents or her foster parents. When Abraham had sent Gabriel to command Markus and his wife Daniela, to raise Adina, Gabriel had never specified whether they should raise her as their child or as a foster child. While this distinction seemed like a trivial matter, it was an explosive one. Markus knew about Abraham's unpredictable and vengeful nature and how easy it was to anger him. Claiming Adina as their child would be stealing the glory from Abraham. However, claiming that she was their foster child could seem derogatory.

Eventually, they told her the truth: that Archangel Gabriel had told them to raise Adina on an order from Grandmaster Abraham. This knowledge had built Adina's ego, and she often reminded her siblings about her special connection to Abraham.

The angel chip gave Adina special abilities. Since Adina had the chip inserted from birth, it integrated well with her brain, which gave her psychic powers beyond those of the other angels. With her ability to control people's minds, Adina was almost impossible to raise as she convinced her parents of her way instead of the other way around.

A unique feature that Adina had, was that she could sense when Abraham tried to read her mind. Adina was the only one on Eden that could control what Abraham saw. Adina became so adept at showing Abraham what she wanted to show him to see that he did not even notice it. Thus, Abraham believed that he could see everything in Adina's mind.

One day, when Adina was seven years old, she scared her foster father Markus. She had made a drawing that was the spitting image of Lucifer. Lucifer was not depicted anywhere on Eden due to the harsh penalties imposed on people associating with him. When Adina spoke, she scared Markus. Her words were: *"Is this, my real dad?*

Chapter 66: Jeshua an Inquisitive Boy.

Jeshua, Lucifer's son, in the foster care of Akiva and Chana, had a childhood that was both similar and different from Adina.

Similar as they stood out from the crowd with their thoughts and behaviour. Different as Jeshua had no psionic powers. Jeshua, being free from the divine technology, could not see the hallucinations induced by Abraham. Being free from the mind control technology he could not understand why people were staring out into thin air reacting to Abraham's speeches. Jeshua had never seen Grandmaster Abraham and the angels impressed him even less.

The Edenites believed that the angels were supernatural beings that served as intermediaries between them and god, but to Jeshua, they looked like men in unique outfits that gave them superpowers. While Jeshua found the Angels' equipment to be super fascinating their personalities bored him. Jeshua thought that the angels were old and boring men who kept repeating the same old lines. On top of that, they took forever to give straight answer.

Fearless and inquisitive, Jeshua almost got in trouble when he asked Gabriel how the angel suit worked. This question indicated that Jeshua did not have a Human chip implanted, as the angels appeared to fly with their wings to the Edenites. Fortunately, Gabriel did not hear Jeshua's question, and Akiva pulled him away before Gabriel noticed him.

Akiva had scolded Jeshua and flogged him for being rude to an angel. Jeshua never understood what was wrong with his question. He was fascinated by the technology behind the angel armour and he wanted to know more. Jeshua realised that Akiva had punished him because he feared the angels. Jeshua concluded that if a big strong man like Akiva, feared the angels, he should stay clear of them as well.

Chapter 67: Adina and Jeshua Meet for the First Time.

When they were 10 years old, Adina and Jeshua met for the first time. It was on 1st of January 2860; or year 50 after the landing. For the Edenites it was also the 50th year in their history. The Edenite calendar followed the Terran calendar out of convenience as Abraham, and his angels had contact with the rest of solar system for supplies.

The New Year's celebration was the largest celebration on Eden, and the population was sitting on different tiers according to their significance. Jeshua was seated at the lowest elevation since his family was farmers. Adina was sitting on the third highest tier since the high priest raised her. Above the high priests sat the angels and on the top level a hologram of Grandmaster Abraham sat on his gigantic throne.

After viewing the spectacle for a while, Jeshua saw Adina. She sat with her family at the high priest's table. They wore elaborate clothing and yet she was the only one that intrigued him. Jeshua felt a hand on his shoulder, and he turned around, it was Akiva.

Akiva:

- Be careful, Jeshua.
- There are terrible rumours about that girl.

Jeshua:

- What rumours, father?

Akiva:

- That she can drive people crazy with the power of her will.

Jeshua:

- But she is just a girl? She cannot be a woman yet?

Akiva:

- In three years, she'll become a woman and you'll become a man.

- That's the most fearsome part. Imagine if her powers grow, as she gets older?

Jeshua:

- But if that is the case, why doesn't Grandmaster Abraham do anything about her?

Akiva:

- We should not interfere with Abraham's plans. Stay away from that girl.

Jeshua:

- Yes, father.

Akiva's warning made Jeshua even more fascinated by Adina. He decided to sneak away and have a look at her when the opportunity arose. A couple of hours later, Akiva got drunk and fell asleep. By this time, most of the adults were quite drunk, and Jeshua snuck up to the priests' tier. He was looking for Adina when someone grabbed his arm. He turned around and there she was, Adina.

Adina:

- Shh, come with me.

Adina led Jeshua behind a tent where they were less visible.
Adina:

- What are you doing here?
- This level hosts the priests' celebration. You're not meant to be here.

Jeshua was lost for words. He had intended to observe the mysterious girl from a distance to satisfy his curiosity. He had not intended to talk to her. Jeshua stuttered:

- I... I was curious about you.
- People say that you are a witch.

Adina:

- I know what people say.
- Ignorant and fearful, they loathe what they don't understand.

Jeshua:

- People are people.
- What don't they understand?

Adina:

- They don't understand reality and the world around them.
- They don't understand the power that I and Grandmaster Abraham share.

Jeshua:

- But comparing oneself to Grandmaster Abraham is a sin.

Adina:

- It is not a sin if you are telling the truth.
- Like Abraham, I can read and influence the minds of humans.

Jeshua:

- Really?

- So, what is my name and where do I come from?

Adina:

- I can't read your mind. You must be unique, that's why I approached you.

Adina's statement confused Jeshua, and he felt reluctant to keep the conversation going. Jeshua tried to defuse the situation:

- Okay, I am Jeshua, son of Akiva. What's your name?

Adina:

- I am Adina, foster daughter of High Priest Markus.

Jeshua:

- Nice to meet you, Adina.
- I must go back to my father now.

Adina:

- I know. We will meet again

Adina watched Jeshua as he snuck away to join his family. The young boy confused her, and he looked like a younger version of her father, Lucifer. She had seen him earlier, and it confused her that she could not reach his mind. Adina had decided to sneak down to study him, but instead, he had come to her. Was this a coincidence or was there a deeper connection between them?

Jeshua was unique because Adina could not read his mind. This fact intrigued her, and she felt compelled to find out more about him. Fortunately, he had told her his name and his father's name. As Adina was influential through her position and unique powers, she would organise so that they would meet again.

Chapter 68: Jeshua and Adina Become Neighbours.

A couple of weeks later, Adina convinced her foster-father, Markus, to offer Jeshua's father, Akiva, employment. Akiva accepted Markus' job offer and Akiva moved to the village with his family. This way, Jeshua became Adina's neighbour so they saw each other daily.

Jeshua wasn't particularly fond of Adina. He thought she was a nosy girl and he felt uncomfortable in her presence. Admittedly, Jeshua had a unique look and he looked more like an angel than a human. However, Adina's attention was not the same kind as the attention he received from other girls. Jeshua couldn't put his finger on why she kept hassling him with questions about his past.

Adina had asked him about his biological father. The question had offended Jeshua. Jeshua had never met his birth parents, and he didn't know anything about them. They died from sickness when he was an infant, and Akiva had taken care of him. Jeshua didn't want to discuss this with his neighbours, and for all practical purposes, Akiva was his father.

However, Jeshua felt grateful to Adina for hiring his dad so that he did not have to grow up in poverty in the desert. Because of Adina, Jeshua didn't have to go to bed hungry, and he also had the opportunity to learn reading and writing.

Meanwhile, Jeshua fascinated Adina, and she suspected that they were siblings. Adina had improved her telepathic abilities so that she could read and manipulate the minds of the angels. When reading their thoughts, she had realised that she was the daughter of Lucifer and an Edenite woman, Sara, who was killed by the angels. Adina did not know how to feel about this, since Grandmaster Abraham was her mentor, while also causing the deaths of her biological parents.

Adina had a clear mental image of the physical appearances of Lucifer and Sara. Jeshua was the spitting image of Lucifer, while Adina looked similar to Sara. Adina realised that there was a way for her to find out if they were related. The angels had an ability that could tell them if two individuals were related. If she controlled the mind of an angel, she could use this ability to find out if she and Jeshua were siblings.

The ability was a form of DNA recognition technology, which was enabled by one of the microchips in the angels' brains. In the past, when the angels were the special operations group for House Goldstein, they sometimes had to solve crimes and find the offender. For this task, they used technology enabling them to "see" the DNA of a person. Using this ability made it easy to find a fugitive in a group of individuals. This ability was operated by smell as the technology could interpret minute amounts of airborne DNA and match it against a database. The signal was transmitted to the consciousness as vision, as it was easier to understand visual information for the human brain. Being a secondary ability, the DNA recognition ability was turned off by default.

While Adina did not know how the DNA recognition technology worked, she soon figured out how she could use it. She focused her telepathic powers, and she to took control of the angel Nuriel. She started by matching herself to herself. The result that was a 100 % DNA match. Her next step was to match her to her foster father, Markus. The result that came up was 0 %. Finally, she compared herself to Jeshua. The result that came up as 50 %. While Adina did not understand what a 50 % DNA match meant, she realised that she was related to Jeshua. After this realisation, Adina sent Nuriel away before he came to his senses and realised that she had a brother.

Chapter 69: The Angels Almost Capture Jeshua.

A couple of years later, it was Adina's 13th birthday, and the day for her adulthood ceremony. Because of Adina's prominence there was a big celebration in the village, and several of the angels were honorary guests. The villagers gathered for the ceremony and Jeshua was sitting in the back row. Abraham gave a lengthy speech projected as an illusion via the divine technology.

Jeshua was sitting in the back of the assembly, and his mind was wandering. Not having a divine technology chip implanted, Jeshua could not see Abraham, so for him these meetings were nonsensical. From Jeshua's point of view, it was a bunch of people staring at nothing and occasionally reciting prayers.

The issue was that Jeshua was supposed to quote the same prayers as the others. Somehow, they knew what prayer to recite from thin air, while he had to catch up every time. Jeshua looked at Adina. It was a strange coincidence that they shared the same birthday. Jeshua had mixed feelings for Adina. He found her awkward, yet he felt a connection to her that he could not understand.

Gabriel and Nuriel stood next to the stage where Abraham was speaking, when Gabriel noticed an anomaly. He whispered to Nuriel:

- Nuriel, how many individuals does your thermal scanners detect in the assembly? Mine says 220

Nuriel:

- Yes, so does mine, what's the problem?

Gabriel:

- How many angels and humans can you detect in the room?

Nuriel:

- 212 humans and seven angels.

- You are right. It shows one angel too many, there are only six of us here.

Gabriel:

- Adina has an angel chip, remember!
- We are missing one human.
- Follow me; we cannot allow non-chipped, non-baptized humans on Eden.

They walked among crowd and they connected with one person at the time. Eventually, Gabriel reached Jeshua. He put his hand on Jeshua's shoulder and he noticed that he couldn't reach Jeshua's mind. He told Jeshua to turn around and was shocked when he noticed that the boy looked like a young Lucifer.

Adina noticed what was happening and she acted quickly. Exerting her powers, she made Jeshua invisible to the angels. Jeshua was confused over what happened. The angel was now looking straight past him as if he wasn't there. He turned around and looked at Adina. She seemed to be in pain and her lips formed the word "run." Adina fainted, and Jeshua used the ensuing confusion to run away from the congregation.

Chapter 70: Abraham Finds Out About Jeshua.

Gabriel:

- I saw him...

- I saw Lucifer, a younger version of him.

Abraham:

- And yet you didn't bring him to me?

Gabriel:

- I am sorry, Master. He disappeared in front of my eyes. One second, he was there, the next he was gone.

Abraham scanned the memories of Gabriel. His archangel wasn't lying, and it was a mystery. Had the young Lucifer been there, or was it a hallucination?

Abraham worried about Adina. Her brain patterns were different from the other angels, and he could not read her mind the same way as he could read theirs. Abraham was unsure whether Adina disrupted what he could see or if her angel chip had malfunctioned. If she manipulated what he could see, she was a threat, but if it happened because of a glitch, it was harmless.

Abraham decided to observe Adina from a distance. In a way, it was a good thing that she hid things from him, as it made his life interesting. Abraham had realised that immortality and full control bored him. It was 13 years since Lucifer's death, the latest event on Eden that had affected him. Abraham realised that one of the underlying reasons for Yahweh's suicide must have been boredom. While Abraham could take measures that influenced the lives of his

Edenite subjects, they had limited consequences for him or the rest of the universe.

Excited that something unusual had happened, Abraham decided to have Gabriel examined. It would take a couple of days, and until then he had some excitement to look forward to, the excitement that uncertainty brought.

Chapter 71: Adina Urges Jeshua to Go into Hiding.

Jeshua sat in the stable and he thought about the day's events. Thinking back on Adina's adulthood ceremony puzzled him. As per usual, the villagers had stared at the empty chair in the middle of the room chanting and showing all kinds of emotions. But during the meeting, the angels had walked around like they were looking for something. This behaviour was unusual as they usually stood stoically and silent during these sessions. Eventually, one of the angels had approached him and stared at him for a moment before acting very weird and staring straight past him. Adina's lips had told Jeshua to run, and she had passed out.

What did this mean? The angel had acted amazed when he saw Jeshua. Why was Jeshua special and why were the angels looking for him? Adina entered the stable and she approached Jeshua.

Adina:

- I have been looking for you.

Jeshua:

- Shouldn't you be resting? It looked like you had a nasty fall when you fainted?

Adina:

- I was pretending to faint as a diversion. It was vital to get you away from there.

Jeshua:

- But why? I am the unimportant son of a poor gardener.

Adina:

- That statement is not true. You are a foster child as am I.

Jeshua:

- Stop telling me that I am adopted.
- Who told you this?

Adina:

- No one did. They did not need to.

- I can read and influence people's minds. Even the thoughts of the angels.

Jeshua:

- Stop that crazy talk!
- Although most people believe that you can do these things.

Adina

- That's because I can. You are the only one that is different.
- Tell me, have you ever seen Grandmaster Abraham?

Jeshua:

- No, I assume he is just a symbol?

Adina:

- NO!
- He is very real, and everyone except you can see him.

Jeshua let Adina's words sink in. He didn't know how to react. Adina was insane, but everything that she said made sense.

Jeshua:

- But. But that can't be, I don't understand any of this.

Adina:

- Let's start over.
- Have you heard about Lucifer?

Jeshua:

- Only in hushed whispers.

- He was a fallen angel who betrayed Grandmaster Abraham, and suffered a terrible death.

Adina:

- That is incorrect. Lucifer was a good man who wanted to do good for the Edenites. Because of this, the tyrant Abraham executed him to set an example.

- He fathered a child with an Edenite woman. I am that child, and I suspect that you are my twin brother.

Jeshua:

- What? Why would you even think that?

Adina paused. It was hard to explain to Jeshua in a way that he would understand. Adina's abilities gave her access to the angels' thoughts and memories, and she knew that Eden and Abraham's divinity was scam. Adina realised that Jeshua didn't have a Divine Technology chip implanted as she could not connect to him. This meant that Jeshua could do, what Adina could not. He could act in secret to bring Abraham down.

Adina:

- Abraham implanted me with technology, so I could read and influence the minds of the Edenites.

- What he does not know is that the technology allows me to read and control the minds of the angels. That's how I found out the truth.

Jeshua:

- And what is the truth?

Adina:

- The truth is that Earth is still around, and the rest of humankind is living in prosperity and freedom.

- The Edenites are a small group of mind-controlled individuals living under the supervision of a deluded psychopath.

Jeshua:

- I am sorry. But I don't want to hear this kind of talk.
- I am not the son of an angel, and all I want is a happy life.

Adina:

- You'll believe me one day.
- Stay clear of the angels. For your safety.

Jeshua:

- Okay, I will.
- Goodnight, Adina

Jeshua walked to the small hut where he lived with his family. He felt confused. He had sought solitude in the stables to clear his mind and Adina's claims made things worse. Jeshua felt that something was wrong with the world and Adina's claims verified this to him.

Jeshua struggled to understand the scope of it all. Adina argued that the world was broken, and that Abraham and was the cause. But what was the solution? Abraham and the angels committed many evil deeds, but they also cured people from ailments, made the crops grow, purified the air, etc.

If they found a way to depose of Abraham, what would happen next? Jeshua believed that Adina would grab power herself, instead of freeing the Edenites from tyranny. Would Adina be a better leader than Abraham? There were many rumours about Adina, and none of them were good. Akiva saw that something was bothering Jeshua and interrupted his thoughts.

Akiva:

- Is something bothering you, Jeshua? You need to sleep early; your adulthood ceremony is tomorrow.

Jeshua:

- Father, why did you tell Adina that I am adopted?

Akiva:

- Why do you ask me that?

Jeshua:

- Adina knew that I was adopted. Yet you told me not to let anyone know about my origin.

Akiva:

- You shouldn't listen to that woman; she is a troublemaker. Adina is messing with people's minds.

Jeshua:

- That did not answer my question.

Akiva:

- I admitted to her that you are not my biological son.

- But we have had you since you were a newborn, so you are like our real son.

Jeshua:

- Did Lucifer give me to you?

Akiva:

- No, we got you from Yehuda. He was a disgraced former high priest who was condemned to toil in the wilderness like we were.

- But he was very old when we got you and he died shortly after.

- But never mention Lucifer again, especially not around angels.

Jeshua:

- I understand, father. Thank you for telling me the truth.

Akiva:

- No worries, son. Now sleep, so that you are fresh for your ceremony tomorrow.

Jeshua's adulthood ceremony took place the day after, and it was a small and uneventful celebration.

Chapter 72: The Wedding Assault.

Three years later, Jeshua still lived in the same village as Adina. He was 16 years old and he worked under his father. Adina had tried to get Jeshua to hide, but he kept refusing.

Jeshua declined for two reasons. Jeshua did not believe Adina's claims about them being siblings and progeny of the late Lucifer. More importantly, he did not escape, as there was nowhere for him to go. Jeshua rather took his chances and stayed in the village rather than living in the wilderness while hiding from the angels.

Jeshua stayed away from the Angels to be on the safe side. It was easy for Jeshua to stay clear of the angels, as they never seemed interested in speaking to him. Jeshua reflected that it was a bit strange as the angels exchanged a few words with most Edenites except for him. This benign negligence changed when Jeshua was 16 years old and attended his brother's wedding.

In the year 2866 Abraham Goldstein instructed the angels to go through the finances of the Edenite population. This review had never happened before as Abraham considered the production output of the Edenites to be insignificant. But the previous year there was a famine on Eden. While the suffering caused by the starvation of 2865 did not bother Abraham, he was bothered because he wasn't the cause of it. If the people were to believe that he was all-powerful, they would believe that he caused the starvation as a punishment. Abraham had struggled to motivate the famine as the Edenites had followed his rules.

To make sure that unintended famines did not occur again, Abraham decreed that the population should build granaries and keep accurate records. When going through High Priest Markus records, Gabriel noticed a discrepancy. He summoned Markus to speak to him.

Markus:

- You summoned me, Archangel Gabriel.

Gabriel:

- I found several discrepancies in your records.
- You paid someone called Jeshua, son of Akiva.
- Do you care to elaborate?

Markus:

- I don't understand what the problem is? Jeshua works for me.

Gabriel:

- The problem is that there is no Jeshua son of Akiva on Eden.

- Everything that is produced on Eden belongs to Grandmaster Abraham, and he shares it with you.

- It seems like you are stealing from Abraham.

- Unless you can come up with a better explanation?

Markus:

- Jeshua exists. I can bring him to you later.

Gabriel:

- Do I look like I enjoy waiting?
- Bring him now.

Markus:

- Well, now is not the right time. Jeshua is attending his brother's wedding.

Gabriel:

- Very well. Lead me to this wedding. This celebration can use my presence.

Adina, who attended the wedding, was drinking wine in a corner when Gabriel and Markus entered. She knew why they were there. However, her intoxication had weakened her psionic powers, so she could not influence Gabriel to leave.

Gabriel approached Jeshua. What he saw shocked him. For the second time, he saw Lucifer's son. The first time, three years earlier, he had disappeared, but this time, he remained in front of Gabriel's eyes. Gabriel decided to confirm the identity of the man in front of him.

Gabriel:

- Are you Jeshua, son of Akiva?

Jeshua:

- Yes, that is me. How can I serve you, Archangel Gabriel?

Gabriel did not respond. He knew what he had to do. For the last three years, he had wondered what he saw at Adina's adulthood ceremony. Abraham had ruled it out as a glitch, and he had declined Gabriel's request to search for Lucifer's son. Abraham needed to see this young man with his own eyes. Gabriel tried to connect with Abraham to share his vision. But this was to no avail, as something was blocking the signal. Gabriel used the built-in communication link in the Angel suit to contact Abraham.

Gabriel:

- Abraham! I have the son of Lucifer at the Gad Tribe Wedding Hall. Requesting instructions.

Since she could not block conventional signals, Adina realised that she needed to act to stop her brother from being captured. Fortunately, the wedding guests were intoxicated and easy to influence. She influenced some of them to stab Gabriel from behind.

The stabbing shocked Gabriel who had not activated the electromagnetic shield that protected his body from attacks. He enabled it as he fell to the ground. The field electrocuted and repelled the attackers, but to no avail. Gabriel knew that he was mortally wounded, and that he couldn't stop the bleeding fast enough. He activated the emergency beacon on his angel suit, closed his eyes and prepared to die.

Having achieved her goal, Adina released the attackers from her psionic control. They realised what they had done and fled the wedding hall before the other angels arrived. Adina caught up with Jeshua outside.

Adina:

- Do you believe me now?

Jeshua:

- What have you done?

Adina:

- I saved you.
- You are my brother, the son of Lucifer, and the saviour of Eden.

Jeshua:

- But you condemned my family. You doomed us all!

Adina:

- Not all of us.

- They will never kill us all. Abraham needs us. Without us, there is no purpose for him to live anymore.

- We will get revenge for our father, but first, you need to hide! Meet me at Gomorrah Cliffs at the southern edge of Eden in one week; I will be waiting for you there, and I will bring supplies.

Jeshua did not question Adina, and he ran for his life towards Gomorrah Cliffs.

Chapter 73: Abraham is Furious.

Abraham looked at the frozen, lifeless body of Gabriel. He was seething with anger but at the same time he felt relieved. Gabriel's murderers had not killed him beyond resurrection. Thus, Abraham could resurrect Gabriel with stem cell grown body parts.

Abraham was baffled when he investigated the perpetrators' minds. They were shocked by the insanity that had led them to kill Gabriel. Gabriel would return to Eden and avenge his own death. This would be poetic justice and it would prove that the Edenites couldn't kill the angels.

Abraham devised a plan. He proclaimed that all the members of Akiva's family would be cast out and killed with fire from the sky within the next year. There they would live in constant fear and see their family members killed, one at the time. This was a glorious plan for revenge and much better than killing them all at once.

The emergence of Jeshua, Lucifer's son, was confirmed by Gabriel's assailants. Jeshua was the perfect likeness to a young Lucifer. Had he incited the people to attack Gabriel? How had Jeshua avoided detection for so many years? Regardless, Jeshua had to be captured, as a he was a threat to Abraham's dominance over Eden.

But it was difficult to find Jeshua. He had no implants so Abraham could not track him, and Abraham had failed to find Jeshua using orbital satellites. To find him without using the satellites was a mammoth task as Eden was 20,000 square kilometres of inhabitable land and he could only commit 20 angels to the search.

Abraham considered commanding the Edenites to find and punish Jeshua. He decided against the idea. Requesting Edenite help, would undermine his claim to be all-seeing and omnipotent. Instead, Abraham chose another course of action. At Mount Sinai, he would force the Edenites to erect a 100-meter tall monument cut into the rock depicting Lucifer's execution, 16 years earlier.

Abraham could have the angels create such a memorial with lasers in a couple of weeks, but he would rather have the Edenites do it with their blunt tools, toiling for ten years to build it. HE was their MASTER, and they existed to SERVE HIM.

Chapter 74: Adina Allies with Jeshua.

A week later, Jeshua met up with Adina in the caves under Gomorrah Falls close to the southern edge of Eden. Jeshua was starving and thirsty as he had had taken detours to avoid the satellite surveillance of Eden. Adina had told Jeshua that satellites were big flying machines that could see him from the sky and report his location to Abraham.

Avoiding the satellite surveillance, was not difficult. Six out of seven suns in the sky was satellites and as a long as the satellites were not within 10 degrees from zenith, they could not see him. So, Jeshua had sought cover every time one of the suns were close to zenith. This was a plodding way to move, as he could only move undetected one-quarter of the time. Jeshua met up with Adina who had brought him supplies.

Adina:

- Welcome to your new home, Jeshua.
- I am glad that you made it.

Jeshua:

- What is this is all about?

- I attended a wedding, an angel approached me, and then the other wedding guests attacked the angel?

Adina:

- You heard what Gabriel said.

- You are the son of Lucifer, the angel who defied Abraham and got executed.

- You do not have a microchip implanted. This means that they cannot control you. That makes you dangerous to them.

Jeshua:

- But you got a chip? So why can't they control you?

Adina:

- I don't know what happened.

- For some reason, they gave me another chip at birth. But that chip gave me unexpected powers. That's why I can enter and control their minds.

Jeshua:

- That makes YOU dangerous to Abraham. Why haven't they come after you?

Adina:

- Because they don't know about my powers.

- I can help our people. If I am detected, we are doomed, and the Edenites are condemned to tyranny.

Jeshua:

- I see
- What is my part in all of this?

Adina:

- Your part is to be the liberator. I will find people who are sympathetic to our cause. You'll meet them and bring them to the edge of Eden. Once you are there, you'll follow the instructions in this letter, and remove their microchips.

- I must return home before someone misses me. Behind those cliffs, there is a network of tunnels that have an almost endless supply of mushrooms. You can stay there invisible to Abraham, together with the people that you liberate.

- I will leave written messages to you under this rock.

After saying this, Adina jumped up on her horse and galloped back home. Fortunately, it took only an hour and a half to race the distance that had taken Jeshua a week to sneak. Adina had no reason to hide. She could move freely and no one would dare to question her. This was because the reputation of Adina's powers had spread across Eden.

Chapter 75: Another Lost Edenite.

Abraham watched Adina performing a religious sermon. He was proud of her. It felt good that his granddaughter was dedicating her life to honour him and his teachings. Adina praised Abraham's benevolent rule with such zeal that Abraham considered elevating her to become one of his angels. He would put that off for a while though and keep observing Adina from afar.

The Abrahameon expressed that only men could be religious leaders, so many villagers objected when Adina became the assistant priest for their village. Abraham had commanded Markus and the gathered congregation that Adina was to be a priest for the village. While Adina's promotion was inconsistent with the earlier message in the Abrahameon, it did not bother Abraham. There were many inconsistencies in the Bible, and if Yahweh couldn't bother being consistent, Abraham didn't need to either.

Accompanying Adina at the altar was the archangel Gabriel and his body-guard, Cherubim. Gabriel's assailants hadn't killed him permanently, because they didn't know about the technology that enabled resurrection as long as the brain had not sustained damages beyond repair.

The Edenites saw the return of Gabriel as proof of his semi-divine status and the ultimate power of Grandmaster Abraham to rule over life and death. Cherubim became Gabriel's bodyguard as Abraham was reluctant to send angels on solo missions after the incident that killed Gabriel.

During the sermon, Abraham was disturbed by a minor notification on the outer edges of his mind. It was a notification that one of his subjects had passed away. With an Edenite population of around 10,000, he got these notifications quite often, so they did not bother him as they were a natural part of life.

In the last year, there was an ongoing issue with people dying, where the body was never found. It had happened again. The latest man to disappear had been a 25-year-old healthy individual. No one had witnessed the fatality, and the surveillance satellites did not cover the place of death. Abraham would send the angels to search for the body, but he already knew the outcome. They would find a pool of blood, but they would not find the body. Since Lucifer's son had appeared a dozen people had disappeared. Abraham concluded that Jeshua was behind the deaths, but what did he want? Refusing to acknowledge his fears, Abraham retreated to the Divine Dimension to meditate.

The mastermind behind the disappearances was Adina who used Jeshua to gather support to overthrow Abraham's reign on Eden. Her method was the following:

Adina used her psionic capabilities to find individuals who were resentful towards Abraham. She told them to wait for Jeshua to set them free. She then rode out to Jeshua's hideout and left a note with instructions on who to release from Abraham and the time and place to do so. Adina made sure that the attention of Abraham would be directed at her for the whole time so that Abraham couldn't intercept the liberation. This procedure also gave her an alibi for every liberated individual, thus putting her beyond any suspicion.

Chapter 76: Abraham Forms a Militia to Stop Jeshua.

With more people liberated, the disappearances accelerated as Adina had more operatives available to free individuals from Abraham's control. Eventually, she grew too bold, and Abraham realised what was happening. For the first three years, Abraham thought that Jeshua killed individuals and hid the bodies. While this notion was unsettling, it did not pose any threat to his power. One event in 2870 made Abraham wake up and realise the danger that Jeshua posed to his rule.

Adina had instructed Jeshua's group to liberate dissenting people in separate locations on Eden at the same time. When people disappeared on the eastern edge of Eden and the western boundary at the same time, Abraham realised that Jeshua couldn't be behind both disappearances. Abraham understood that Jeshua did not kill the disappearing individuals, he liberated them. In return, they helped him in his underground rebellion against Abraham.

Abraham checked a map of Eden's maintenance tunnels and he realised how blind he had been. All disappearances had happened close to the entrances, which explained how the liberated individuals could disappear without a trace. Abraham's first impulse was to gather his angels and order them to search the tunnels.

Abraham realised that this was not the best course of action. The tunnels were vast and covered hundreds of kilometres. Jeshua, might have set traps the tunnels while waiting for the angels to make a move. While it shouldn't be possible for an Edenite man to kill an angel in a battle outfit, Abraham would not underestimate the man who had stayed hidden for three years while snatching Abraham's subject one by one.

Instead, Abraham chose another solution, one that required patience, time and manpower, factors that Abraham had in abundance. He would raise religious militias that would guard the entrances to the maintenance tunnels. This way, the rebels would eventually starve to death and they could no longer re-cruit any new individuals for their cause. If the blockade made the rebels come out and fight, then Abraham and the angels could kill them quickly out in the open.

Abraham added a passage to the Abrahameon that stated that the entrances to the maintenance tunnels had to be guarded.

The corruption of Lucifer's soul was so endless that the destruction of his body was not enough to put him at rest. Instead, the spiteful energy of Lucifer's lost soul made its way to the deepest pits of hell where he was tormented for eternity while calling out for other evildoers to cometh and join him. To stop this evil, Grandmaster Abraham commands that all the tunnels leading to hell need to be guarded. As evil stems from man's weakness, Man must defend against it and be vigilant. So sayeth the wise Grandmaster Abraham.

After a couple of weeks, Edenite militias blocked all the entrances to the maintenance tunnels, which made it impossible for Jeshua and his rebels to move in and out of the tunnels undetected. Now Abraham could wait and bide his time.

Chapter 77: The Destruction of Jeshua's Militia.

Jeshua looked at the tunnel exit and saw that an Edenite militia blocked the path. He sighed. He and his rebel group had been stuck down in these catacombs for a month. Although they had access to mushrooms and water, it was not sustainable to stay in the darkness indefinitely.

The only light source in the tunnels was from the luminescent paint with directions visible every 50 meters. Apart from this bleak light, they were in complete darkness. They needed to find a path to the surface as soon as possible.

Jeshua looked at the guard post in the distance. It was guarded by six men. These men would not be a match for Jeshua's group. But, Jeshua suspected a trap. There would be angels waiting for them, and the six men at the guard post were a bait to lure them out. Jeshua told his followers to find an unguarded exit, but they did not listen to him. They had been stuck in the darkness for a month and all the exits were guarded. They needed to get out to avoid going insane from the darkness.

Adam, one of Jeshua's followers, pushed Jeshua to the ground.
Adam:

- I have had enough of this, Jeshua. I didn't join the rebellion against Abraham to cower in these dark, bloody tunnels to the end of my days.

- You got us down here, and now we are stuck here because of your cowardice.

- This is our chance, there are only a few of them, and there are thirty of us. Let's get out and get us some proper food.

Jeshua:

- Shut up, Adam.
- They have set a trap for us. We need to...

Adam sucker punched Jeshua in the head. Unprepared for the strike, Jeshua fell backwards, hit his head on a rock, and fell unconscious.
Adam:

- The craven fool that got us here is dead.

- Let's save ourselves by getting out of these damn caves. Let us get us some warm food and some warm cunt.

The group murmured in acknowledgment. Most of them had been miserable since Jeshua "freed" them. They had suppressed their misery by telling themselves that they were winning. It had felt that way, when they increased their numbers from the ever-watchful eyes of Abraham and his angels. But they had never had a long-term plan; at least they had not been aware of the long-term plan.

To defeat Abraham, they needed to take the fight to him. It was time to fight Abraham. United behind Adam, the group charged the guards to break free.

The Edenite militia took up their weapons and prepared to fight the enemy, but Abraham instructed them to drop their weapons and run out in the open. The militiamen dropped their weapons and ran as fast as they could. Once Adam's men were out in the open Abraham released the trap. Firstly, he set off the explosives at the entrance to collapse the tunnel so no one could get back in. Then he killed the rebels using the orbital laser cannons he had at his disposal. A couple of minutes, later they were all dead turned into a jumbled mess of blown up body parts and burnt flesh.

Chapter 78: The Search for Jeshua's Body.

Abraham enjoyed studying the carnage. It felt good, putting these insolent rebels into place using his superior weaponry. He would instruct the Edenite population to make a pilgrimage to Gomorrah Cliffs so that they could witness the punishment that befell upon anyone who rebelled against his rule. There was, however, one thing that bothered him. The angels were unable to locate Jeshua's remains.

Abraham contacted Gabriel who was analysing the battlefield:

- How is it going?
- Have you found any trace of the traitor yet?

Gabriel:

- Analysis from our orbital satellites and the remains found on the ground, indicate that we killed 30 collaborators in the battle.

Abraham:

- That is good news, but I am asking about Jeshua.

Gabriel:

- We have found no evidence for Jeshua's death. However, the battlefield is contaminated so we cannot rule out that he is among the fallen combatants.

Abraham paused. There had been 30 mysterious disappearances related to Jeshua in the last four years. There were 30 slain rebels outside the tunnel entrance at Gomorrah Cliffs. Had Jeshua sacrificed all the insurgents to fake his own death? Or was his body to be found in the tunnels? Regardless, without his men, he proved no danger to the angels and Abraham ordered a search for him.

Abraham:

- Gather the angels and search the tunnels for Jeshua. Be careful they might have set traps for you.

Gabriel:

- Understood, I will clear this entrance and approach the tunnels from here. I will instruct others to search from the other entrances.

A few hours later, Jeshua woke up after being unconscious for over 24 hours. He was disoriented and could not recall what happened. He was alone in the camp, and there was no one else to be found. He felt weak but he got up on his feet. Jeshua remembered Adam punching him, and he realised that he needed to stop the others from leaving the tunnels.

Going out as a group was the equivalent of suicide, and he had to stop them. Much to his dismay Jeshua realised that the entrance was caved in. He had arrived too late to save his group. This realisation filled Jeshua with despair. Jeshua could see the angels clearing the cave-in. He headed back to camp to find a hiding spot. Jeshua could only think of one location where they wouldn't be able to find him, the latrine. He jumped into the latrine, closed his mouth, and struggled to not vomit as he was floating in excrement. The angels Gabriel and Thomas entered the camp.

Gabriel:

- Thomas, what do you see?

Thomas:

- Not much. It is quite dark in here.

Gabriel:

- Try DNA detection and heat signature.

Thomas:

- His DNA is all over the place, but mostly from the latrine. The same thing goes for the heat signature.

Gabriel:

- It sounds like you're on latrine duty, Thomas.

Thomas:

- Ha-ha very funny, Gabriel. Do you think Abraham will be pleased over me wading around in shit, wearing a 3 million Terran Credit battle suit?

Gabriel:

- I would find it funny to watch.
- Very well, just go there and have a look.

Jeshua heard that Thomas approached the latrine. He closed his eyes, held his nose, and dropped under the surface.
Gabriel:

- What do you see?

Thomas:

- Shit, Shit and wait, more shit.

Gabriel

- Fire off a few rounds to be sure.

Upon hearing this Jeshua sunk to the bottom of the latrine. Thomas fired off a multitude of shots, which would have hit and killed Jeshua if it wasn't for the high density of the excrement. Instead, the bullets disintegrated, and the kinetic energy from the bullets splashed up as a shit, hitting Thomas who wasn't amused.

Thomas:

- Fuck you, Gabriel! You knew that was going to happen, didn't you?

Gabriel:

- So, should you. All these years of training back on Earth and yet you forgot why spear guns are used instead of high-powered rifles underwater.

- Let's move on

- You search the southbound tunnel, while I search the northbound tunnel. We'll meet here in three hours.

The Angels' left and Jeshua released all the vomit he was holding in. His first instinct was to get out of the latrine, but he realised that if he did, he would spread excrement all over the camp. and the angels would know where he was hiding. Instead, he bided his time until the angels had left the tunnels. Jeshua was amazed that the angel's weapon didn't kill him. He saw this as a sign from Yahweh, the true god, that his time would come to overthrow Abraham.

Jeshua had a bath in the camps water source. While it was a shame to destroy the camp's water supply, it did not matter anymore. His followers were dead, and Jeshua was going to hide somewhere else. There was enough mushrooms and water in these tunnels for Jeshua to sustain himself while waiting for a sign from Yahweh that he should rise as the saviour of the Edenites.

Chapter 79: A Few Years Pass.

The following years, Jeshua waited for a sign from Yahweh. The sign never came, and instead, Jeshua wallowed his life away in the darkness. He passed his days having vivid hallucinations induced by the darkness and psychoactive substances in the mushrooms he ate. Jeshua became sickly and he grew a massive beard and long hair. One day, two years later, Jeshua regained his mental clarity and he knew what he had to do.

Meanwhile, Adina strengthened her powers. Adina pretended to be Abraham's strongest advocate. She succeeded Markus, and became the high priest for her tribe. Using her psychic powers, Adina influenced the other high priests to appoint her to the newly created role of Grand High Priestess and she ruled all of Eden. To appease Abraham, she ordered the Edenites to build a giant monument at Mount Sinai commemorating the defeat of Lucifer at the hands of Abraham. Adina reckoned that the best way to prove her loyalty was to create a monument that celebrated how Abraham had killed Lucifer.

Adina was biding her time. Her capabilities got stronger every day, and she learned how to control the angels from several kilometres away. She had to be careful and hide her intentions. Although Abraham could not send an angel to kill her, he could use the orbital laser cannons to do the job. Adina knew that Abraham always had a laser cannon aimed at her, as one of the seven suns followed her around, while the other six stars were moving in a pattern over the sky as time was passing.

Being followed by an orbital laser, Adina could not search for Jeshua and influence him to rebuild his militia. She was uncertain whether he was alive, although she knew that the angels had not found him on the battlefield at Gomorrah Cliffs. Adina wanted to look for Jeshua, but she could not move freely without creating unwanted attention. Adina hoped that Jeshua would seek her out, but it never happened.

Abraham Goldstein was impressed by his granddaughter. Adina had achieved things that were beyond his greatest imagination, and she used her talents to honour him. Abraham could never have asked for a better progeny, and he finally had a descendant who made him proud. Abraham also feared Adina. She was powerful, and Abraham feared her reaction if she found out the truth about Lucifer. This was Abraham's conundrum. On the one hand, he wanted Adina to know that she was his blood, but on the other hand, he feared how she would react if she found out the truth. Adina was Lucifer's daughter, and Abraham and had brutally executed Lucifer.

Abraham believed that Adina could control what he saw when accessed her mind. Every time Abraham accessed Adina's mind, he found praise and love for him and his actions. Everyone feared and loved him to various degrees, but only Adina showed a one-sided love and admiration for him. Abraham didn't buy it. Adina would have her doubts and fears, just like everyone else, so why couldn't he detect these emotions?

It also occurred to Abraham, that the angels acted strange around Adina, as if she controlled them. Abraham decided to take precautions to keep Adina under his control. To keep Adina in place, he programmed one of the orbital lasers to follow Adina around, so he always kept her supervised.

Two years later, in 2872, events unfolded that would change the fate of the Edenites forever.

Chapter 80: A Zetan prophecy.

Ra, Zeus, and Brahma were observing the Divine Palace in the Divine Dimension. The Zetans had been locked out from the Divine Palace for eons after Yahweh created a dimensional rift that barred them from entering. With their home planets destroyed they could not power up their other portals back to the regular universe. The materials needed were inside the Divine Palace, which was behind the dimensional rift. They had tried to communicate with Yahweh, but there was no sign of life from their old companion who had betrayed them and barred them from the palace.

The Zetans concluded that Yahweh was dead, because otherwise, they could detect his life force. For the last century, they had sensed a human presence in the Divine Palace. They had concluded that this human was not physically in there but he had managed to transport his mind to the Divine Dimension. While this was an impressive technological feat, it would not help the Zetans. They needed someone to physically enter the Divine Dimension to bring them back. Besides, the human that lived in the Divine Palace was uncontactable via telepathy, and he could not help the Zetans.

While Abraham's presence in the Divine Dimension was unwelcome, the Zetans were still excited over their prospects. If humanity had managed to send a mind to the Divine Dimension, they could activate the portals on Earth.

There was a human that the Zetans could communicate with across the dimensions. That woman had psionic capabilities they had not encountered in centuries. This woman had what her predecessors lacked; she had access to technology that would enable her to open the portals, so the Zetans could travel to Earth and once again become the masters of the galaxy.

It was time for the Zetans to act. The Zetans were a bit anxious as opportunities like this did not come around that often. While they could not KNOW the future, their highly advanced brains enabled them to make accurate predictions that would increase the likelihood of success. They gathered in a ring, interlocked their arms, and brought themselves into a trance so they could communicate with their human host.

The Zetans disconnected with their host. Soon, the future would be theirs.

Chapter 81: Jeshua Comes to a Sudden State of Clarity.

Spending two years in solitude, in the dark tunnels below, Eden drove Jeshua insane. Fear drove him, and he felt that someone was looking over his shoulder at every turn. Since he hadn't interacted with other humans for two years, he had lost his ability to communicate, and he spent his days walking around in the tunnels hissing at imaginary foes and living on mushrooms and water. Jeshua's insanity made him forget who he was or where he was. He reeked and he hadn't shaved nor cut his hair for two years.

Suddenly, Jeshua came back to his senses. He knew who he was and what he was meant to do. He went back to the abandoned camp at Gomorrah Cliffs where he bathed, shaved, and changed his clothes. He went to the tunnel entrance and waited. He sat there quietly and at peace. His time to make a difference would soon come.

Chapter 82: On the Run.

Keila Eisenstein was looking in a pair of high-grade binoculars through the rear window of the *"Miss Freedom"* spaceship that she commanded. Things looked bleak for her rebel group, The Martian Humanist Alliance. They had narrowly escaped a Terran Council expedition that destroyed their base "Freedom First" on the Asteroid Sylvia. Unfortunately, they were pursued by Keila's arch enemy, Rear Admiral Bjorn Muller, onboard his command ship "ISS Supreme Earth"

Inspired by her mother, Susanna, Keila had joined the Martian Humanist Alliance, a rebel group that smuggled supplies between poor worlds to help them circumventing the Terran Council trade monopoly. The Terran Council trade monopoly kept fringe worlds destitute while amassing wealth to the wealthiest families on Earth. Keila looked at the picture of her mother, which she had in a necklace hanging around her neck. Keila missed Susanna, but this was not the right time to mourn her. Her crew needed her, and they were far from safe.

Keila closed her eyes, and she saw how the wounded Susanna was sucked out into the vacuum of space after a missile hit her asteroid base. Keila trusted her vision. Although she had not seen it happen with her own eyes, she knew that the vision was telling the truth, her premonitions always were.

Keila closed her eyes and she hoped for insight on how to get away from the pursuing ship. She saw nothing and she felt despair. Was this the end, or would she figure something out? The premonitions had helped her countless times to escape overwhelming odds. That's how she had become a hero for the down-trodden and the most wanted on the Terran Council's elimination list. Since she could only see the death of her mother, Keila opened her eyes and tried to figure out a solution. The situation was dire:

- Her ship was slower than Bjorn's, so she could not outrun him.

- Her ship was unarmed, so she could not fight him.
- There were no friendly colonies nearby so she couldn't hide from her enemies.

Keila closed her eyes again. Her mother spoke to her in a vision *"The time has come... The time has come to save Eden from the tyrant Abraham."*

But what did this vision mean? Susanna had told Keila that she grew up in a world without technology, which was governed by a dictator who claimed to be God. But there was no place called Eden in the solar system and Susanna had refused to take Keila there. Keila had never believed in the existence of Eden. She knew most of the ins and outs of the solar system, and she had never heard about such place from anyone else but her mother. *"But the vision has to mean something,"* Keila thought and she summoned her co-captain Sven to discuss their options.

Keila:

- How does it look. Do you have any reports from the Freedom First base?

Sven:

- No. We must assume that the base is destroyed. You saw the armada they sent to kill us.

Keila:

- My hopes and prayers are with our allies that were there.

Sven:

- Hopes and prayers don't win wars. Actions do.

Keila:

- I never wanted this war. I wanted to set things right. I hoped that we could live in peace and harmony.

Sven:

- Well, our enemies saw things differently.

- Have you made any plans yet, or are you still waiting for your *"pre-monitions"*?

Keila paused. She did not like Sven's scepticism, but she could empathise with it. Sven was rational and a highly skilled pilot, but he lacked imagination and divine inspiration. She understood that her gift was beyond most people's understanding.
Keila:

- My mother spoke to me.
- It is time for us to save Eden.

Sven:

- Are you serious? We are in the middle of a crisis, and you are bringing up your mums' childhood story?

Keila:

- Don't you dare to call my mother a liar after everything she did for you!

Sven backed down. This was not the time to argue. Besides, Keila and Susanna had saved them many times in the past.
Sven:

- I apologise Keila.

- I did not mean that Susanna was a liar.

- I think she had a traumatic upbringing and Eden was her coping mechanism.

Keila:

- Apology accepted.

- Now, look at this map of this part of the solar system. If Eden existed, where do you think it would be?

Sven:

- Nowhere.

Keila:

- Not helpful, Sven. What about B528A & B528B

Sven:

- Research stations claimed by House Goldstein
- Most likely hostile.

Keila:

- House Goldstein? They are not part of the Terran Council, are they?

Sven:

- They used to be. They were the mightiest faction on Earth at one stage, but they declined after the death of Abraham Goldstein. Eventually, they lost their seat on the Terran Council and House Bolivar replaced them.

Keila:

- Hmm. Abraham Goldstein...
- Susanna mentioned freeing Eden from the tyrant Abraham.
- B528A must be Eden.
- Set the course for Eden, Sven.

Sven:

- I am not sure about this...

Keila:

- You don't have to believe, Sven, just do.

Sven:

- Understood, Keila.
- I have set the course for B528A.

Chapter 83: Keila is Crashlanding on Eden.

12 hours later, Miss Freedom was outside Eden. It was ominously quiet as they drove past Eden. There were weapon systems in place, but they were not communicated with nor fired at. Keila entered one of the emergency pods on the Miss Freedom. The crew had refused to land on the asteroid, as it seemed like their pursuers had given up their pursuit. Sven had tried to convince Keila to not go to Eden, but she had stood by it. Her visions had told her that it was time to save Eden and she had more faith in her sights than she had in Sven and the rest of the crew. They parted ways, and Sven gave her a radio transmitter with a reach of 1/3 astronomical unit (50,000,000 kilometres), so she could communicate with a friendly vessel when she needed to be picked up.

Keila looked at Miss Freedom as her emergency pods made its way to land on Eden. Suddenly, she saw something that terrified her. Bjorn's command ship approaching from the blind side on top of Miss Freedom. Keila pulled up her radio to warn Sven and the crew but it was too late, and moments later Miss Freedom was eviscerated by the direct fire from the enemy ship. Panicking to get away, Keila disengaged the safety switch on her escape pod and she crash landed on Eden. Her escape pod crashed close to Gomorrah Cliffs, and she lost her consciousness upon impact.

Chapter 84: A Warship at the Gates.

Abraham was meditating when Nuriel tried to reach him. Abraham entered Nuriel's mind to see what he saw, and it was troubling news. Outside the Divine Control Centre, there was a Terran Council warship as well as the debris of another ship.

Abraham panicked; had the Council sent the army to stop him? If they had, that would be the end of him, as the remnants of House Goldstein would not come to his defence. Abraham calmed down. He was on a well-armed battle station more than capable of taking out a single warship. The Terran Council knew this, so if they had come after him, they would have come in force and not with a single ship.

Abraham decided to communicate with the vessel over the hologram generator. Abraham spoke through Nuriel, as his robotic body would not be well received.

Abraham (Via Nuriel's body):

- Rear Admiral Bjorn Muller, you have entered and discharged your weapons in a restricted area, state your business.

Bjorn Muller:

- The Terran Council is the rightful owner of the entire solar system. So, restricted areas do not concern us, Nuriel.

- We have destroyed a hostile ship in this area. The hostile ship belonged to the infamous criminal Keila Eisenstein.

Abraham:

- Very well.

- You shouldn't have intruded. I can assure you that we will file a complaint with your superiors.

- Now leave and let us deal with the destroyed ship.

Bjorn:

- I am afraid that leaving is not an option.

- We believe that Keila escaped the ship and landed on the surface of B528A. We will not leave without apprehending her.

- We will send down our men to find her.

Bjorn's attitude angered Abraham. He was an intruder who stepped in and started making demands. Abraham couldn't allow Terran Council officers to land on Eden to look for a suspect. In the Abrahameon, Abraham claimed that Earth was destroyed and the people on Eden were all that remained of humanity. Having foreign troops with advanced technology looking for a rebel would crush the illusion of Abraham's divinity. This would sow dissent that was unstoppable, even with the powers that the divine technology chip gave him.

Abraham aimed all the orbital lasers at Bjorn's ship and spoke:

- I won't allow that. Eden is private property and not under the authority of the Terran Council.

- This was decided on the Terran Council meeting in 2785. It will stay this way in perpetuity.

Bjorn:

- Are you out of your mind?

- You are threatening a Terran Council command ship. Attack us, and the entire fleet will come after you!

Abraham:

- Yes. But you will be dead long before they get here.

Bjorn:

- This is unacceptable!

Abraham:

- Your intrusion on my private property is unacceptable.

- But I will let you live if you stand down.

- Move your ship to the dark side of Eden. I will send men looking
for the fugitive.

Bjorn Muller turned silent. Abraham's attitude perplexed him and he did
not know how to continue. If Bjorn ignored Abraham's warnings and sent men
looking for Keila, it could lead to a fatal confrontation. But Bjorn could not
back down, as he had to look after the reputation of the Terran Council. Bjorn
found a middle ground.
Bjorn:

- I will give you three days to deliver Keila to us. If you don't, we will
attack.

Abraham:

- Very well.
- We will sort this out. Now get your ship to the dark side of Eden.

Abraham watched as the Terran Council warship travelled to the dark side
of Eden. He would contact the Terran Council and ensure that this troublemaker was sent home and reprimanded. Abraham would remind them of the
agreement made back in 2785 when Eden was awarded the status as his domain
for perpetuity.
While this problem was averted, the worst problem was still there. An outsider was running around with critical knowledge and modern technology on

Eden. He needed to wake up all the angels and send them to find and eliminate this outsider before she caused any more issues.

Chapter 85: Panic on Eden.

Meanwhile, the Edenites was panicking and believed that the end was near. They had seen the explosion in the sky when Keila's ship blew up. It was clear to them that something was amiss when six out of seven suns stopped shining and instead illuminated the alien spaceship in the sky. The turning of the orbital lasers caused the surface of Eden to have a sudden and frosty night while the alien spaceship was illuminated and highly visible. Eventually, the suns came back, and the foreign ship disappeared, but the event had caused significant doubts among the Edenites, and chaos ensued.

Adina saw her chance to get away from the satellite that followed her. She knew that she would not be the first thing on Abraham's mind, and this was the opportunity that she had waited for. Adina got on her horse and galloped to the closest entrance to the maintenance tunnels. She needed to use this window of opportunity to find her brother. Adina entered the tunnels. The tunnel networks under Eden were vast, but she was confident that she would discover Jeshua. Providence had caused the explosion in the sky, and it would lead her to Jeshua. Together, they would find a way to depose of Abraham, so that she could rule Eden.

Chapter 86: An Otherworldly Beauty.

Jeshua heard a loud bang close to the tunnel entrance at Gomorrah Cliffs. He felt a moment of fear; had the angels decided to come after him again? Jeshua ignored the fear. Fear had kept him down in the dark for the last two years, and it was time to act. If death had come for him, he would accept it, and if it were his salvation, he would embrace it. Regardless, it was no longer time for him to hide.

Jeshua exited the tunnel and saw the crashed wreckage. It looked different from anything he had seen on Eden, although the technology reminded him of the angels. He remembered what Adina had told him; that Earth was still around and that there lived humans there. Was this some of these humans, and why had they come?

Jeshua opened the hatch to the wrecked escape pad. Inside the escape pad, there was an unconscious woman, who was the most beautiful woman he had ever seen. She looked so different from all the other humans on Eden, and her clothes and hairstyle were different. She was an otherworldly beauty. Jeshua gave her a gentle pat on the shoulder. She did not respond. Was she dead? Jeshua touched her throat to feel her pulse. She had a weak but stable pulse.

Jeshua realised something. That one of the suns would soon be straight on top of them, and when it was, Abraham would find out about them and send his angels to kill them, or kill them outright with his orbital lasers. Jeshua had seen people being murdered by the suns in the past as it was one of the favourite ways for Abraham to kill people; incinerating them with a hot beam of concentrated sunlight. Jeshua gathered his strength and he lifted Keila out of the escape pod. After that, he dragged Keila to the relative safety of the tunnels.

Half a minute later, the satellite discovered Keila's escape pod, which let Abraham know about her location. He sent Gabriel and Nuriel to investigate as the other angels were still being revived from the cryogenic sleep and they were unable to act until they had recovered.

Chapter 87: A Cave of Carnal Desire.

Keila was returning from unconsciousness to a dreamlike state. She had another vision. In the vision she had seductive and erotic sex with an athletic stranger in a cave, with a ring of fire around them. The sex was pulsating and getting stronger and stronger until it climaxed, and she woke up.

To Keila's surprise, she woke up in a cave looking at a stranger. This stranger was not as attractive as the one in her visions. His facial features were similar, but he looked sickly and malnourished. Was this man a friend or a foe? He was definitely not an officer of the Terran Council armed forces. But who was he, and what was this place? Everything in the cave looked ancient, and she had no idea why they weren't using electric lighting to make the area more liveable.

Keila recalled what her mum had told her about Eden. It was a terraformed world that housed a strange cult, living as people did in ancient times. The cultists worshipped someone called Grandmaster Abraham. Keila had assumed that this was one of her mum's made up childhood stories. But the visions had led her here, and she could only do what they showed her.

She closed her eyes again. *"Follow the vision,"* she thought. She did not know why she was getting visions, but she knew that they were of divine origin. While she had preferred to be able to choose what premonitions she would see, she could only make the best of God's plan for her life. She got the erotic vision again. She hesitated a bit; the man in front of her wasn't attractive in real life. Then again what damage could it do to her? Maybe the reason for her to have sex with the man was not for her pleasure, but to get ahead. She would do what needed to be done, to get rid of the tyrannical cultist Abraham.

Keila looked at Jeshua again. She could tell that he was bursting with sexual desire. Keila decided to go for it. The visions told her to have sex with the stranger, and she would rather be in control of her life than being raped. Jeshua reciprocated, and they had sex. It was all over after a couple of minutes. Keila sighed of relief. The sex was mediocre, but it had relieved her stress. She realised that she hadn't slept much lately and that the crash had injured her. She leaned back and fell asleep in Jeshua's arms.

Chapter 88: Adina Intervenes and Saves Jeshua.

Jeshua looked at Keila, who slept on his shoulder. She was beautiful and mysterious. They hadn't spoken much before she seduced him. It had surprised him, but it was a welcome relief from the fear and paranoia that had dictated his life. Jeshua had accepted that he was going to die today, so he had followed his curiosity and investigated the crash. He had uncovered this angel sent to him to show him paradise.

Jeshua had never been with a woman before. Was he in love? He wasn't sure. The Edenite way was all about loving and worshipping Grandmaster Abraham. The union between man and woman through marriage was necessary for procreation, but the emotions between them were inconsequential. While Jeshua was an active opponent of Abraham and his teachings, he had never reflected on the emotion of love and attraction before, so he did not know his position on the subject. All he knew was that he had found paradise between Keila's legs and that he wanted to return there as soon as possible.

Jeshua looked up and he realised that he was in trouble. Gabriel and Nuriel stood next to his bed, looking down on him Keila. Realising there was no point in resisting or trying to escape he pulled Keila towards him and hugged her. If he was going to die, he wanted to die in her arms. He took a deep breath. He was ready. But the shot never came. He looked up again; the angels were still standing there, unaware of his location, staring straight through him. He looked at Keila. she was awake, trembling with fear. Jeshua heard the angels speak.

Gabriel:

- What is happening, I can smell him from this bed, but I can't see him

Nuriel:

- Maybe the foreign bitch brought some form of cloaking device?

Gabriel:

- That's a negative. I have scanned all the different spectrums, and I would have detected them.

Nuriel:

- Just shoot the bed then.

Gabriel:

- True.

As Gabriel pulled up his weapon, Keila dragged Jeshua out of the bed. They ran into the tunnels while Gabriel was shooting the bed to pieces.
Nuriel:

- Did you get them?

Gabriel:

- That's a negative; there is no blood beside the smell of them is gone.

Meanwhile, Adina observed the angels through their eyes. It was a close call, and she was happy that she had accessed their minds when she had. Through her ability to control their minds, Adina had controlled their vision so that they couldn't see her brother Jeshua and his mystery woman. Fortunately, her brother had made a run for it instead of being pulverised by the multitude of bullets destroying the bed he lay in.

Adina felt frustrated that she had entered the tunnels from the wrong part of Eden. She should have realised that Jeshua would come back to the caves near Gomorrah Cliffs. That part was his "home," and that's where he had spent most of the time since he went into hiding from Abraham and his goons. But she could not foresee things or empathise with people in a usual manner. Her special powers made her able to see and know everything a chipped person saw or understood, but this gift also made her blind for how non-chipped people were thinking. This inability was not a big issue on Eden, where everyone had a divine chip implanted at birth, but it had made her unable to understand her brother. She contemplated to find her brother and his mystery woman, but she decided against it. The tunnel networks under Eden where widespread and she was 50 kilometres away from his position. Finding him in the dark was like finding a needle in a haystack. Besides, there was another more urgent reason. Abraham would soon start looking for her, and when he found her, she was better off being a good girl spreading his word than a rebel lurking around in the dark tunnels under Eden.

Adina made her way back to the surface and she rode back home. She was thinking of the half-naked mystery woman that she had seen through the eyes of the angels. Who was she? Adina knew that an intruder had crashed on Eden and that Abraham was desperate to find and detain her. The foreign whore had not wasted any time in seducing Jeshua, but what was her endgame? Was she a potential ally or was she worth more as a tribute to Abraham?

Adina realised that she had the means to find out, while still showing her friendly façade to Abraham. Her psionic powers had grown so much so that she could simultaneously control a multitude of humans. So, all she needed to do was to send them to look for Jeshua. If she found Jeshua, she would speak to him through her host, and if the humans were detected and killed by Abraham, there was nothing that bound them to her. Adina got home and went to the meditation room in the temple she was supervising. Unlike the angels and Abraham, she could control humans directly. She did not know why this was the case, but she knew that neither Abraham nor the other angels were able to do so. Adina went into a deep meditative state. She needed to pinpoint and influence the humans around the tunnel entrances to search for Jeshua. If she did, one of them would find Jeshua, and she would establish contact. It was a dangerous move for the humans that she influenced as entering the tunnels were prohibited to the Edenites. Then again, for Adina, the individual humans of Eden were expendable; while she did not seek to punish and torment them, she did not care if Abraham did it, if they could serve her cause.

Chapter 89: Abraham Gives a Fatal Order.

Abraham:

- It's all on the video captured by your helmet cameras.

- They were right in front of your eyes; you were staring at Lucifer's son and his foreign whore for ages, and you did nothing. Then they get away, and you start shooting at their bed! Explain yourselves

Gabriel:

- I swear to you, Grandmaster Abraham. We could not see them. We could smell them, but we couldn't see them.

- Eventually, we shot their bed as we deemed that they might be using some form of cloaking device to stay out of sight.

Abraham:

- Well, you should have shot when they were still there.

- You are supposed to be elite soldiers. Yet you could not see two important fugitives in front of your own eyes.

- They were not even using any cloaking device. They are visible on your helmet camera, which is filming the visible spectrum of light.

- Next time, use your instincts. if you can smell them, shoot them!

Gabriel:

- Yes, sir

Abraham:

- Dismissed, angels!

As the angels left the room, Abraham took a seat in front of a computer terminal. He had chosen not to punish them for their failure. He lacked in manpower, and he had realised that they told him the truth. They were, in fact, unable to see Jeshua and the foreign woman. The big question was why they couldn't see Jeshua and Keila. Someone was manipulating their cognitive capabilities. But who could it be? Abraham had experienced similar episodes in the past, where angels had blacked out for no apparent reason.

Could Adina be behind it? She had stronger psionic powers than the angels, despite having the same chip implanted.

What made Adina an unlikely culprit, was her intense zeal for Abraham and his ideology. She was his strongest advocate on Eden and the only one on Eden, who showed no doubts in trusting his intentions. But was this her real feelings? Abraham felt like Adina was directing him and showing him what he wanted to see instead of what she really felt. This seemed implausible as the god chip was meant to have total access to the thoughts and senses of the people connected to a lower tiered chip. Abraham decided that Adina was not the one sabotaging him and that he was doing him a disservice harbouring paranoid thoughts about his granddaughter when there was a real threat on Eden, Keila.

Being cut off from House Goldstein, Abraham did not have detailed intelligence reports about Keila Eisenstein, but there was plenty of information on the Spacenet. Keila was one of the leaders for the Martian Humanist Alliance, a revolutionary group who fought for the downtrodden and hated the Terran Council's dominion over the solar system. Despite her young age of 22 years, Keila had reached the top 10 list for people chased by the Terran Council, and there was a 10 million Terran Credits bounty on her head. Nothing of this explained what she was doing on Eden, but then Abraham saw who Keila's mother was.

Susanna had been a unique offering as she had volunteered to be selected. This behaviour was against the rules, but as they had received a high offer for her, they went ahead and sold her off to Mahmoud Rashid. Abraham tried to recollect what else had happened on that day 32 years ago. He realised that they had forgotten to erase Susanna's memories and disconnect the divine technology chip from her brain.

Susanna knew everything, and if she knew the right people, she might have figured out how to remove and reverse engineer the divine technology chip. That would explain why her dangerous daughter had landed on Eden, and it also confirmed Keila's reason for coming

Fortunately, Keila had lost the rest of her crew when the Terran Council destroyed her ship. Keila didn't any weapon, otherwise, she would have attacked Gabriel and Nuriel. Although she managed to stay hidden from the angels' vision, she could not mask her scent. Abraham would use this to his advantage. He contacted Gabriel:

- Gabriel, I have a task for you

- Lead a group of four angels to the tunnels at Gomorrah Cliffs. Shoot at anything that smells like Jeshua or Keila. Let's flush these bastards out.

Gabriel:

- Copy that, sir. I will gather a group and move at once.

Chapter 90: Keila Sets a Trap.

Keila was staring into the ceiling with Jeshua on top of her pumping her rhythmically. It was not very enjoyable, but it was not the end of the world either. Throughout her life, she had been tortured by Bjorn Muller and other criminals, having sex with an unattractive man was not a big deal. She felt perplexed that Jeshua was thinking about sex when they were chased by armed men. Jeshua seemed so beguiled by her as if he had never been with a woman before. No matter, Jeshua was her ally for now, and she needed allies to get away from this place alive, especially with the Terran Council on her trail. She could feel him coming, and they could now focus on the challenging task at hand.

Keila:

- Feeling better now, big boy?

Jeshua:

- Yes. I feel like I am in heaven. I have been waiting for you all my life.

Keila:

- Me too

Keila forced herself to smile before changing to a more serious tone.

- But for us to stay together, we need to find a way to kill those men before they kill us. Then we can leave this place.

Jeshua:

- No there is no need for that, we can hide. I know these caves better than they do, so they will never find us. There is enough mushrooms and water for us to live here in peace while Abraham can rule over the surface dwellers.

Keila:

- But don't you want to come with me and see my home? It's a lot cosier than these damp tunnels.

Jeshua:

- Your home?
- Don't you live with Abraham and the angels in the Divine Control Centre?

Keila decided to play along to see if she could get Jeshua to comply.
Keila:

- Yes, I do.
- How did you figure that out?

Jeshua:

- Because my sister told me that the angels were not gods, but men.
- Men need women. Thus, there must be women at the Divine Control Centre.

Keila:

- Yes, you and your sister are brilliant.

- The male angels are the mean bullies, and the female angels are lovely.

- If you help me take control of Eden, things will be a lot better. You'll be able to live on the surface with your friends in peace and harmony.

Jeshua:

- I used to have friends.

- My sister directed me to people who were like me.

- We lived together in the caves like family.

- But then my sister wanted to fight Abraham, so my friends went out to fight. They all died, and left me alone in the tunnels.

Keila:

- Well, I am not your sister.

Jeshua:

- Yet you want the same thing. You want to fight Abraham and steal his power.

Keila:

- And what do you want?

Jeshua:

- I told you already. I want to stay here with you.

Keila started to get frustrated with Jeshua. If he was not going to be helpful, she was better off ditching him and figuring this out by herself. Then again, Jeshua seemed gullible, stupid, and out of touch. Keila decided to make one last attempt at playing it nicely before telling Jeshua to get fucked.
Keila:

- I would love to stay here with you, but I can't.

- You see; I need angel food that I can only find up in the sky; otherwise, I will die.

Jeshua:

- My sister never told me about angel food. I think you are lying.

- However, I was ready to die today. Yet, here I stand, united with the most beautiful woman in the world.

- I'll do your bidding.

Keila:

- I am glad to hear that, Jeshua.

Jeshua:

- So, how do you plan on killing the angels?

Keila:

- Well, I noticed they could smell us, but they couldn't see us.

- Their commander is going to believe that we are wearing an experimental cloaking device that hides our visuals. So, with that in mind, he is going to shoot at our smell signature.

Jeshua:

- What does that even mean?

Keila:

- If they can't see us, they will shoot at things that smell like us. If we can make them smell like us, they might shoot at each other.

Jeshua:

- How are you going to do this?

Keila:

- Just listen, and I will tell you how this is going to play out.

After that, Keila described how she was going to lure the angels to kill each other. It was an intricate and challenging plan, but it was the only option they had on hand. Keila had recognised the armour and weaponry that Gabriel and Nuriel had. They wore mechanised suits with thick armour that was impenetrable with the primitive weapons they had on hand. The mechanised exoskeleton also made the angels powerful, and with quick reflexes that made it impossible to overpower them. Their only chance was to make the angels kill each other. Fortunately, There was a reason why Keila was the most wanted individuals in the solar system.

Chapter 91: Abraham Notices That People are Flocking to the Tunnels.

The days after the appearance and destruction of the spaceship around Eden, The Edenite society descended into chaos. Fear and confusion spread among the population as the appearance of other humans contradicted the claim in Abrahameon that Eden was the last bastion of humankind. What made the chaos worse was that Abraham's religious scriptures were focused on control through fear, power, and obedience, so softer values like love and compassion were not emphasised. Thus, when there were doubts about Abraham's powers, the Edenite society spiralled down to chaos, with murders, looting and rapes at an endemic level.

Abraham did what he could to stop the chaos. As it turned out, he could not do as much as he wanted. While Abraham could kill all the wretched sinners, this was not a practical option as that would kill off most of the population and would leave him with very few subjects to rule.

The problem was that he had controlled his subjects through fear and control, and when there were doubts about his powers, the fabrics of society collapsed. At that stage, he only had direct authority over the angels, and they only numbered 20, in comparison to the over 10,000 humans on Eden. The temple guard and the religious militia had disbanded, and they were contributing to the chaos instead of quelling it. Since a few angels were needed to control and support the Divine Control Center, and a few were needed to hunt to down Keila, that meant that only a handful of angels could be spared to police Eden and try to restore order. Since Eden span over 30,000 square kilometres, this was a mammoth task.

Fortunately, time was on his side. As soon as he had captured Keila and got the Terran Council off his back, he would have all the time in the world to restore order on Eden.

When Abraham scanned through all the humans connected to the divine technology, he noticed that many of them were exploring the maintenance tunnels that was running below the surface of Eden. His first reaction was rage and fury. Humans were forbidden to enter the maintenance tunnels as they *were the gateway to hell"* and he wished to punish all the offenders. But then a pragmatic thought dominated his mind: that the humans walking around in the tunnels would help him to find Keila. He decided to watch them from afar to see how their venture into the tunnels played out.

Chapter 92: Adina and Jeshua Prepare to Strike Against Abraham.

Eventually, one of the humans roaming in the maintenance tunnels came across Keila and Jeshua. Fortunately, Adina noticed their presence first. Adina took control over Elizabeth and spoke through her.

Adina:

- Jeshua and Keila. Don't be afraid. Your sister is talking through me.

Keila to Jeshua:

- What's with that woman? I have never seen anyone with an expression like that, she looks like a zombie.

Jeshua:

- My sister has extraordinary powers. Let us see what she has to say.
- Thank you for contacting me, sister. It has been a long time.

Adina:

- Yes, two years

- I could not contact you as you don't have a divine technology chip implanted, and I did not want to send others looking for you as that would endanger you.

Jeshua:

- So why are you contacting me now?

Adina:

- The arrival of your special friend has plunged Eden into chaos.

- The Edenites saw the other spaceship destroyed with their own eyes. That proved that Abraham was lying, that the people on Eden are not the only ones left of humanity.

- We have been planning to free Eden from Abraham for five years. There won't be a better time than now.

Jeshua:

- I agree. We have a plan in place.

Adina:

- Tell me about it?

Keila:

- I don't know you, and I am not sharing my secrets with a stranger.

Adina:

- Fine, then I won't help you.

Jeshua:

- Please sister, Keila is just a bit on edge after everything that has happened to her. Any help would be much appreciated.

- We plan to kill Gabriel and Nuriel who was lurking around in these tunnels before.

Adina:

- They still are, they are down here with two others. About five kilometres away.

Jeshua:

- We only planned for two angels Can you distract the other two?

Adina:

- I'll see what I can do.

Jeshua:

- Good.
- The trap is around here. Can you alert them to our position?

Adina:

- I will release my control over Elizabeth. Then Abraham will know
where you are and that you are unarmed. That would lure them
straight in.

Jeshua:

- Excellent, you should do that.

Adina:

- Farewell, until we meet again.

Adina released control of Elizabeth who panicked and started screaming in
terror. Abraham noticed her elevated emotional state and rejoiced at what he
saw. His decision to not punish the sinners who had ventured into the tunnels
had paid off, and he now knew the position of the fugitives and that they were
unarmed. He would send his strike force to intercept at them. To stall their escape, he would send this frenzied woman to attack them. She was, after all, expendable.

After a short struggle, Jeshua and Keila subdued Elizabeth. They left her tied up and gagged but conscious. They stayed close to her to give Abraham a false sense of security before carrying out the ambush.

Chapter 93: A Two-Front Attack.

Adina noticed that the pursuing four angels were only three kilometres away from the position of Jeshua and Keila and they were approaching quickly. Although they were on foot, the top running speeds of angels were over 60 kilometres an hour due to electrical stimulation from the exoskeleton suit. Hence, they would reach Jeshua in a less than three minutes. Adina did not know the details of Jeshua's plan, but she knew that it was meant to kill two angels, and she had promised to distract the other two. Adina took a deep breath. She realised that if they failed today her life would be over. In a way, it was strange that Abraham had not killed her already, as he had no trouble killing people that he perceived as threats.

At the surface, the angel Eremiel was giving out instructions to the religious militia on how to restore order to their village. Adina focused and sent the army into frenzy. To Eremiel's shock they jumped him and pulled his weapon out of his hand and tried to shoot him. This attempted attack was unsuccessful as the activation code for the weapon was in Eremiel glove, and the gun wouldn't fire without it. Eremiel tried to fly off, but the weight of the humans trying to pull him down stopped him from lifting. Eremiel activated the electrical field on his combat suit and electrocuted the attacking militia men. However, enabling the electromagnetic field short-circuited his suit as it had taken blunt damage from the army beating him with their primitive weapons.

Eremiel felt weak. Since the electrical circuits broke, he was carrying a cumbersome suit unassisted. He got up on one knee. He was looking at the angry mob a few meters away from him. A few of them lie dead on the ground burnt from the electrocution, but the others were just even angrier. He contacted all nearby angels for immediate evacuation.

Gabriel picked up the transmission as he was passing in the tunnels below Eremiel. He ordered the others to stop.

Gabriel:

- Eremiel is in danger. Haniel and Hamshal, go to the surface and help him fend off that peasant mob.

Haniel:

- Master Gabriel, Abraham ordered us to focus on killing the two fugitives.

Gabriel:

- Let me and Nuriel deal with them. They are unarmed and they should not pose a threat.

- Eremiel is in danger. We can't allow a peasant mob to kill one of our own.

Haniel:

- Understood, sir

Having said this, Haniel and Hamshal rushed to the surface where the militia mind-controlled by Adina, had set a trap. As they rushed up from the tunnels, the army set them on fire through pouring olive oil over them and setting them alight. Haniel and Hamshal whose armours were still intact were protected by the built-in cooling in the armour, while Eremiel was roasted in his outfit. Abraham decided to control the two angels directly. Focusing his efforts on Haniel and Hamshal, he lost vision and focus on Gabriel and Nuriel who had reached their targets in the tunnels below.

Meanwhile, Gabriel and Nuriel caught the vision of Jeshua and Keila. They were running separate ways into different tunnels. Gabriel and Nuriel split up to run after them. After a short dash, Gabriel reached a platform with a smoke-filled smelly cave below. The smoke was so thick that he couldn't see anything in there. He could not smell Jeshua or Keila either. Suddenly, he heard a call "now" and they hit Gabriel with a container filled with a liquid. After that, he could see that smell signature of Jeshua appearing on the other side of the room. He remembered his orders, raised his weapon and fired off a multitude of bullets.

Gabriel realised that someone had shot him. He slumped down to the ground. The last thing Gabriel saw was Jeshua's face before everything turned black.

Everything had gone according to plan. After Keila and Jeshua's first encounter with the angels, Keila had predicted that they would fire at their smell signature if they were to meet again. She had been fighting and evading the Terran Council's strike teams for years, and she knew what technologies and tactics they were utilising. By making sure that the angels smelled like them, Keila tricked them into shooting each other. To make sure the angels smelled like them, they had filled two small clay containers with their own blood and sealed them, to create a blood-filled container that would splash upon impact. They had chosen the place for the ambush carefully. They set up the ambush in a cave with two different paths leading to two different platforms overlooking the cave. In the cave, there was a type of mushroom that gave off a very thick and smelly gas that would block the angels' vision and would mask Jeshua's and Keila's smell. Once they threw the blood containers, this smell was strong enough to be picked up by the angels' enhanced senses tricking them into shooting each other.

Keila got dressed first. The angel suit she got from Nuriel's corpse was too big for her, but it was still operational. She made her way Jeshua who was struggling to open the suit and get Gabriel's dead body out of it. With Keila's help, he was done in a couple of minutes. Jeshua's suit was also operational.

Keila:

- We better hurry!

Jeshua:

- To do what? We have weapons and armour now. We can fight them here if they dare to come down.

Keila:

- No, we'll take the battle to them, that's the only way!

Jeshua:

- That's suicide; the orbital lasers will shoot us down.

Keila:

- I know what I am supposed to do here. I am going with or without you.

Jeshua:

- I am coming with you! I don't want to live without you.

Keila:

- I am happy to hear that.
- Providence will make us win this battle.

After saying this, Keila and Jeshua rushed to the nearest exit. Once they reached the surface, they began their ascent to the Divine Control Centre.

Chapter 94: Adina Distracts Abraham.

Abraham could feel a sharp pain when Gabriel and Nuriel died. Through a strange twist of fate, however, he did not notice their deaths, as Eremiel died at the same time. Moments later, the orbital lasers came into position and Abraham wreaked havoc on the rebels. They tried to flee when they saw the fire coming down from the sky, but Abraham left them no quarter, and killed them all.

Abraham saw the battlefield through the eyes of Haniel, and it was a scene that broke his spirits. His entire religious militia lay dead on the field. There were 250 dead men, men who were meant to do his bidding on Eden. Eremiel was dead beyond resurrection burnt to the bone. Without human troops, he would not be able to restore Eden to order in years. His number of angels were dwindling, and they were not easy to replace. Abraham considered killing everyone on Eden and start over. It was easy to do. If he deactivated the nanotechnology layer that covered Eden, its atmosphere would leak out in space, as Eden's gravity was not strong enough to keep an atmosphere. Without an atmosphere, every living being on Eden would die within minutes. Abraham stopped himself. He had invested so much time and money to create Eden. It was too laborious and demoralising to replace its entire population with new subjects.

Instead, Abraham focused on getting the culprit behind the chaos, and he had a clear suspect, Adina. By backtracking the connections of the fallen men on the battlefield, the conclusion was clear: Adina was to blame, and she was a lot stronger than Abraham had predicted. He contacted Adina. To his surprise she allowed him to connect with her mind. Abraham studied her position. She was sitting in the open on a cliff at Mount Sinai overlooking the landscape. Adina was a sitting duck for his orbital lasers; all he needed to do was to get them in position.

Abraham started speaking to Adina to distract her and stop her from running for safety. The orbital laser would be in a striking position within 10 minutes.

Abraham:

- Adina, my dearest granddaughter, what have you done?

Adina:

- You have never called me granddaughter before.

Abraham:

- You know who you are, so why hide it from you any longer?
- I know your secrets as well; you have been hiding them well.

Adina:

- I am sorry for the families of those men. Unfortunately, the fight for freedom often comes at a steep cost.

Abraham:

- Freedom...

- Do you know how easy it would be for me to wipe out every living being in this world by letting the air out in the vastness of space?

- Tell me, why should I let the others live after I kill you?

Adina:

- Well knowing you.

- Compassion, common decency and humanity are out the window.

- I would say your reason for not killing everyone is because you are powerless without subjects. Without them Eden is just a worthless piece of rock.

Abraham:

- You are indeed my granddaughter. A shame your traitorous nature will earn you the same ending as Lucifer, your duplicitous father.

Adina:

- Knowing this, what stops me from hiding in the tunnels as my brother did?

Abraham:

- If you do, I will drain Eden's atmosphere killing you and everyone else.
- I will not share power with you after your betrayal.

Adina:

- Fair enough. I suppose I'll sit here for the next few minutes until your laser gets in position. And then we'll see if you have what it takes.

Abraham:

- You'll see, and you'll feel. I'll give a painful death you, damn traitor!

Adina looked up at the sky. She could see one of the suns/ orbital satellites moving closer to zenith above her. Once it reached the peak of the sky her life would be over. Unless Jeshua and Keila managed to get into the Divine Control Center and kill Abraham before that happened. It was not likely to occur, but it was her only hope. Adina felt calm and collected, her entire life had come to this. Now all she could do was to distract Abraham for a few more minutes hoping for the best.

Chapter 95: Entering the Divine Control Centre.

Keila looked up ahead at the asteroid that hosted the Divine Control Centre. It was less than a kilometre away, and she hoped that she could make it that far. She was in incredible pain. The bullet holes in her angel suit were small, but they were big enough to let in the freezing and low-pressurised air from space touch her body. The cold was not the main issue, but the low pressure was. Even the smallest breath she took expanded her lungs like a balloon and caused severe pain. If she made a medium sized breath, her lungs would burst, and if she disconnected her air supply, she would suffocate. She looked at Jeshua, just behind her; he seemed to be struggling even more. She had received simulated training for this kind of scenario, while all he had received was her quick instruction *"Only shallow breaths, otherwise your lungs will burst."* They reached the airlock entrance to the space station. Keila prayed to The True Maker that she would not face a difficult security system at the gate. She didn't. The only security was a camera that scanned the code on her helmet. A display showed "Welcome back, Nuriel" and she and Jeshua could enter the airlock. The air became pressurised, and they could draw full breaths, resting exhausted on the floor.

Abraham got shocked when he saw a notification that Gabriel and Nuriel had entered the Divine Control Centre. He tried to connect with them, but there was no connection, only a prompt saying that the subjects were dead. Abraham had forgotten about them for the last 30 minutes, and he realised that Adina had tricked him. He contacted Adina with one final transmission:

- You betrayed me. The foreign whore is here because of your deception. Now you'll all die.

Abraham set all the orbital lasers to target Adina, and he also set the nanotechnology layer protecting Eden's atmosphere to turn off in 10 minutes. If he were to die, they would all die. He then took control of the angel Abaddon. Abaddon was one of the most fearsome fighters he had left, named after the angel of destruction in the original holy book. What he lacked in personality, he made up for in destructive capabilities.

With the destructive capabilities of Abaddon, Abraham subdued Keila and Jeshua by shooting them in the legs and arms. Abaddon walked up to Keila to shoot her in the head with his pistol when Adina intervened. She tried to take control of Abaddon and make him kill himself. Abraham noticed this and they wrestled for authority over the angels with their minds. Eventually, the struggle became too much for them, and they both got knocked unconscious from the psionic blast that occurred. Adina's fell backward off the ledge she was standing on. This fall happened at the same time as the orbital lasers were fired at her, effectively saving her from getting hit. She fell for 50 meters and landed in a hole where the laser could not hit her from orbit.

Keila looked up; and she saw Abaddon who lay dead next to her with a hole in his head. She looked at Jeshua, who was injured but alive. They got out of their broken angel suits and they crawled to the room next door where Abraham's brain and his robotic body connected to the particle accelerator that transferred his mind to the Divine Dimension.

Chapter 96: Jeshua Confronts Abraham in the Divine Dimension.

Jeshua:

- What the hell is that thing?

Keila:

- That is the brain of Abraham Goldstein, inserted into a life-supporting robot.

Jeshua:

- I don't know what that means.
- How do we kill it and save my people?

Keila:

- To kill Abraham, you'll have to travel to the Divine Dimension and kill him there.

Jeshua:

- Okay, how do I do that?

Keila:

- I'll help you.

Keila closed her eyes for a moment. Like she expected the vision for how to continue, came clearly to her mind. It had seemed to be like that all her life:

When Keila closed her eyes, the answer would come. She plugged in Jeshua to the particle accelerator and sent his mind to the Divine Dimension.

Jeshua woke up in the courtyard of the Divine Dimension. The place was quiet as if time stood still in there. Jeshua looked around; he saw an old man with a robe and cane sitting still under a lotus tree. Despite never seeing Abraham before, Jeshua knew that it was him. He approached the old man.

Jeshua:

- Abraham! Stand up! It is time for you to pay for your crimes.

Abraham stood up.
Abraham:

- Jeshua right? We meet at last. You are an elusive character.
- You look a lot like your father.

Jeshua:

- I never knew my dad, but I know what is right.

Abraham:

- Please tell me, Jeshua. Who decides what is right?

- Your father decided your fate when he chose to hide you from me.

- Then your sister decided your fate when she used you to rebel against my rule to put her in power because she couldn't do it herself.

- And finally, your newfound "love" decided your fate when she sent you here to face me. Tell me, how do you think you'll get out of here?

Jeshua:

- They did what they thought was right. That's the difference between you and them.

Abraham:

- No. You see, I also do what I think is right. Doing what one thinks is right is not a correct measure of morality. Most people can justify their actions somehow.

Jeshua:

- And how do you justify your actions, you mass murdering monster?

Abraham:

- Easy. I did what I did because I was meant to do it.

- For thousands of years, humanity followed gods. I did too. Yahweh was the god of my people. A good god that gave us morality and a purpose for living.

- But Yahweh was a deception. He was an alien of an advanced set of species from another planet. He was a Zetan.

- When I came here, he had already committed suicide.

Jeshua:

- How does any of this justify your actions?

Abraham:

- You see, Yahweh was never a god. However, humans believed him to be a god because of his superior technology.

- Through providence, I found this technology. I spent my wealth creating a world where humanity could believe in something again. Believe in me.

- I created a world where men could believe in something that was greater than themselves, just like Yahweh did.

Jeshua:

- But they don't follow you out of love. They follow you out of fear. People need freedom to be happy and thrive.

Abraham:

- Freedom?

- The last few days of utter chaos and destruction can be categorised as freedom. I don't think it made anyone happier.

Jeshua:

- Because people lack love. Edenite society is not based on love. It's based on rules and commitments.

Abraham:

- Soon enough, love will be the least of their problems. Air, on the other hand, will be their problem.

Jeshua:

- Why is that?

Abraham:

- Because I turned off the air supply to Eden when I knew I was defeated.

- Within 5 minutes the Edenites will suffocate and die. While you are stuck here with me.

Jeshua:

- No, because I will kill you first.

Jeshua jumped on top of Abraham and delivered a hard flurry of punches to his face. Abraham hit him with his cane, and Jeshua flew several meters. He looked at Abraham in awe.

Abraham:

  - You don't seem to get it. Your body is not here, only your mind.

  - We can keep punching each other until the end of times, until we get out or our bodies die.

Jeshua:

  - Is that so?
  - Your head doesn't look that well.

Abraham:

  - That bitch, she killed us both

Jeshua got surprised when he looked into a well to see his reflection. Abraham was right; he also had blood flowing out through a hole in his head. Jeshua fell to the ground, and everything became dark.

Keila put down the smoking gun. Killing Jeshua had been difficult but necessary. Keila had never included Jeshua in her long-term plans, and her visions had shown her that she was meant to get rid of him in the end. She had hesitated to pull the trigger on him when he was unconscious and plugged into the particle accelerator.

Keila had wanted to say good-bye and tell him why he had to die, but she couldn't do it that way. In the few days, they had been together she had grown connected to him, and she did not know why she had to kill him. Keila swallowed hard and tears ran down her cheek.

Keila pulled herself together; this was not the time to be weak. Keila entered a command on the computer terminal to reactivate Eden's atmosphere. She locked the doors and had the particle replicator create a new divine technology god chip. Keila would have to wait for a couple of hours for the particle replicator to create a new god chip. Once she had inserted the god chip in her brain, she would be in control of Eden, and she would not settle for this small rock. She had bigger plans for the solar system.

The story continues in "The Divine Sedition"

| Page

Don't miss out!

Visit the website below and you can sign up to receive emails whenever Martin Lundqvist publishes a new book. There's no charge and no obligation.

https://books2read.com/r/B-A-QIOG-TWYT

BOOKS 2 READ

Connecting independent readers to independent writers.

---

terious divine connection. Her visions are leading her way, and with access to the late Abraham Goldstein's technology, Keila can unveil secrets that will help her free humanity from the oppression of the few elite plutocrats dominating all of humankind. But, her connection comes at a price. Thus, are the Zetans, controlling Keila as a puppet, indeed better than the Terran Council oppressors she seeks to replace?

Read more at martinlundqvist.com.

Also by Martin Lundqvist

Divine Space Gods
Divine Space Gods: Abraham's Follies
Divine Space Gods II: Revolution for Dummies
Divine Space Gods III: Rangda's Shenanigans

Sabina Saves the Future
Sabina's Pursuit of The Holy Grail
Sabina's Quest to Open the Portal in the Sun Pyramid
Sabina's Expedition to Stop the Apocalypse

The Divine Zetan Trilogy
The Divine Dissimulation
The Divine Sedition
The Divine Finalisation

Standalone
Matt's Amazing Week
James Locker The Duality of Fate
The Portal in the Pyramid
Money Laundering in the Laundromat
Pyramidportalen

Matts Fantastiska Vecka
Divine Space Gods Trilogy
Sabina Saves the Future: Complete Trilogy
Diez Historias Aleatorias y Muy Cortas
Ten Random and Very Short Stories
Dieci Storie Casuali e Molto Brevi
Dix Histoires Aléatoires et Très Courtes
Zehn Zufällige und Sehr Kurze Geschichten
Cinco Historias Aleatorias y Muy Cortas
Five Random and Very Short Stories
The Fall of Martin Orchard
Masa Depan Putri Sabina
La Caída de Martin Orchard
The Banker and The Dragon

Watch for more at martinlundqvist.com.